ALL THE WAY

By

Loraine Haynie

And God said to man "…. what doth the Lord require of the, but to do justly, love mercy and to walk humbly with thy God."

Micah 6:8

Acknowledgements

Putting words on paper has been my joy since I was eleven years old. A seventh grade school assignment to write a short story and then read it to the class started my love of making words come to life on paper. When the class was disappointed at the end of my story and asked for more, I knew that I would always love the process of creating.

However, the act of writing, creating and developing characters sometimes overshadows the technical aspects needed to present the work in written form. Like overlooking the flaws in a loved-one, sometimes the flaws in the written word are unconsciously overlooked with the writing and editing. Thankfully, I have friends who graciously accepted the "job" of pouring over this creation and identified errors and unclear sentences or paragraphs.

A new friend, Betty Smith, was my first reader and encouraged me to continue the process of completing my work. I am so thankful for her love and support. Two dear friends from twenty years of working, sharing, crying and laughing together agreed to be editors for me.

Fran Fields, an avid reader and experienced editor graciously agreed to take on the challenge. She used her keen eye, skill in grammar, and hunger for a good story-line to pin-point, identify and correct the manuscript.

Anita Scott, also a proficient editor, voracious reader, and lover of words and how they flow to pull you into the story was also eager to be part of the process. She gave guidance in areas that were unclear and praise in areas that painted a clear picture for her and made her feel a part of the story.

There is no greater gift these two dear friends could give me than to be a part of this project. I love them dearly. Of course, my husband, Billy who turned his television down occasionally, left the room often, and watched me labor over this creation for hours, days, weeks and months deserves praise for his patience and support. He always has my love.

Preface

When you look into the dark brown eyes you see beauty and depth, but you also see sadness and caution. This is the way she lived most of her life.

In those early years, there was music, laughter and family. Then there was shame, shunning and family division. But there was always love. Family bonds were stronger than any outside disapproval. Until it wasn't.

That's when meeting a gentle, kind, dark haired, handsome man changed her life. But even his love did not completely erase the years of feeling ostracized.

ALL THE WAY

She is running, getting closer now. She can feel the coolness of the tree branches shading her path. She raises her arms to her head. Both of her hands grip her black, curly hair as if to tear it from its roots. She can't breathe. Then her scream starts. She falls to the ground and curls into a ball.

When Ola wakes, it is late afternoon. There are no sounds. The headaches come so unexpectedly and crushingly. But she is accustomed to that. What is different today is the cause of the headache.

She slowly uncurls herself and rises to her knees. "Dear God let this be a dream. Please don't let this be real. I must get back to the house to start dinner. The younger children will wonder where I am." She drags heavy limbs and pounding head into the sunlight and immediately squints to block the blinding rays. Each step almost knocks her to her knees. She has had migraines all of her adult life and knows she should lie down in a dark room to alleviate some of the nausea, but that is not possible with eight children and a hard-working husband expecting dinner in an hour.

As she approaches the back screened door and sees Peggy curled up in a chair, knees up to her chin, tears streaming down her face, she sighs. "My precious Peggy. How do I comfort her? How do I tell Papa? He adores her." Henry always favored Peggy out of his four daughters. She was slender with long blonde, wavy hair and clear blue eyes. She knew how to nestle in his lap, put her arms around his neck and tell him how much she loved him. Martha was the oldest and the strongest, most assertive of his daughters. While he loved her and admired her moxie, he couldn't get close to her, hampered by the wall she hid behind. Susan was outgoing and loved everyone. Her bubbly nature lit up the room when she entered. And sensitive Kathryn was shy and withdrawn, but kind and encouraging to others. Her bobbed-off brown hair and dark brown eyes gave her an innocent appearance. That's why everyone called her Kitty.

The boys were quite different. Earl, Frank, Ralph and Bill were handsome, each in his own way. They were competitive but would defend each other if an outsider wanted to cause harm or embarrassment. They were becoming men and felt the power and adventure that distinction gave them.

They were a musical family and an active part of the First Baptist Church. The boys, except for Frank, played on the school baseball team. All Frank wanted to do was play his trumpet or guitar. He'd written several songs, though he hadn't told anyone about it. He wanted to be a musician when he left home. He wasn't sure how that would turn out, what with the country deep in the Depression now. But he was hopeful.

It was a happy time for the family. Papa had been lucky to land a job as a horticulturist with a large mill in the small town of Covington. Jobs were scarce these days during the Depression. The pay wasn't much, but the mill provided them with a home. The school was within walking distance as was the mill. Mama stayed home, raised the kids and kept the house running. She knew how to stretch a dollar. They had a small garden in the back yard for tomatoes, cucumbers, green beans, squash, okra and watermelon. She made the girls dresses from flour sack cloth. She mended socks, cut cardboard to cover holes in shoe soles and gave her tithe to the church. They would make it through this hard time and land on their feet again. The main thing was that they were together as a family. Many men had to go across country to find work, leaving wife and kids alone to manage on the money they were able to send home.

Mama let the screen door close softly and walked over to Peggy. She couldn't hug her and tell her everything would be okay. She was too angry now. Tomorrow would be time enough to offer her compassion. Tonight they had to face Papa. She didn't see Kathryn come around the corner of the house. "Get up and go wash your face. We will have dinner as we always do. Then you, Papa and I will go out to the back yard and talk."

Kathryn wondered at Mama's harsh voice toward Peggy. Mama never spoke with that tone. Kathryn stood still until Mama opened the door and went into the kitchen. Then she quietly went back to the front yard. She had seen Mama run to the woods, hands in her hair and knew that Ola was having one of her migraines. Usually, the girls would tend to dinner when Ola was racked by the torture of the headaches.

3

And then they would put cool cloths on her head as they helped her to bed, closed blinds and kept the house quiet. By the next morning Ola would be fine and life would resume as normal. Tonight Mama went to the kitchen to put final touches on dinner and was able to hide her pain until bedtime.

Peggy hadn't seen Kathryn either. She sat for a few minutes on the porch, wiped her eyes dry and did as she was told. She wanted her Mama's arms around her, but she knew they had to be strong tonight. If Mama hugged her, they would both fall apart and be unable to carry on through dinner.

Kathryn went through the front door and quietly entered the kitchen. "Need any help Mama?" She knew that it was a struggle for Ola to function with the pain and she couldn't bear to see her like this. She loved her Mama more than anything in the world. She knew how much Ola did for the whole family each day without any concern for her own needs and desires. Kathryn hoped to one day be a mom just like Ola—soft spoken, kind, God-loving and generous to a fault. She jumped in and grabbed plates and flatware for the table and in a few minutes had everything set up for dinner. She talked softly to Ola about her day at school so that she wouldn't jar her nerves with loud noises. Then she went to the parlor to wait for the boys to come in so that she could warn them to avoid horse-play during dinner so they would not cause extra pain for Ola. She saw it as her job to take care of her mom when no one else saw the need.

2.

"Mom, let's go outside and see the courtyard. It looks lovely from here. The garden benches are placed where you can enjoy the encore azaleas, crepe myrtle and bedding plants. The walkway is flat and easy to maneuver your walker around." Loraine tried to sound upbeat and encouraging.

"There's no use doing that. I won't be going outside much. I'll be afraid I might miss your visit if I'm not in my room," Kathryn countered.

"You won't miss my visits Mom. I'll come find you. There are not a lot of places to look. But here you have someone to give you your medications, bathe you and fix all your meals. They do your laundry and clean your 'apartment'." Loraine was careful to use the word apartment, so that it wouldn't seem like Kathryn was giving up so much. "I know where the game room is for bingo, card games, and craft classes. And the music performances are in the lobby, movies and Sunday worship are in the chapel. You'll be so busy you won't even know I'm not around."

"I don't care about those things. Just be sure I have plenty of books. I'll just sit in my room and read or watch TV."

Loraine tried not to grit her teeth. Here's the old guilt trip again. Didn't Mom understand that there was no way she could handle all the personal care her Mom needed now. The bathing and dressing was one thing, but the incontinence was way beyond her physical ability to manage. Even though Mom was a slight 118 pounds, Loraine was 60 years old herself. Lifting 118 pounds was out of the question for her. She had told herself that she would never put Kathryn in a nursing home, that she would find a way to keep her mom with her and Billy, a place Kathryn considered her home. But unintentional as it was, it had to be done.

She feigned a smile and hugged Kathryn. "Mom, you know we wouldn't be here if Billy were not sick. You've alternated living with us, Janice and Dan and Don and Teresa for the past five years. You would still be doing that if Janice wasn't taking care of Dan during his cancer treatments, or if Don could retire, or if I could be sure we would not be in the hospital for days after Billy's surgery."

"I could stay by myself at your house." Kathryn offered.

"No, Mom. It would not be safe. If I'm at the hospital for days there would be no one to cook for you, give you your meds and be near for you to shower. I would be broken-hearted if you fell or got hurt some other way when you were alone. This is not a decision we wanted to make, and Billy feels so bad that his illness is causing you to move."

"I know. I just want to be with my family. I don't know anyone here." Kathryn's eyes filled with tears.

Loraine's heart felt heavy with guilt and sadness for her Mom. "It is a beautiful place and the staff seems so loving and kind. We've bought you bedroom furniture, curtains, and picture frames filled with pictures of your children and grandchildren. You have our recliner and a new TV. It's a cozy apartment and beautiful. I love you Mom. I'll come as often as I can. You're only 45 minutes away. Please try to be happy here."

She leaned over, kissed Kathryn and quickly turned around to hide her tears. When she got to the door, she looked back and waved. "See you real soon. Love you!"

Billy was waiting at home for her to go with him to the surgeon. So, there was no time to linger, worrying about Kathryn's situation. She knew her mom would be safe and taken care of. It would be up to her to make the best of her new living arrangement. Loraine tried to reason with herself. It didn't work.

Kathryn had always been a soft-hearted, loving mother. Her family was her whole world. She wanted to be with them every minute of every day, especially after Loraine's Dad passed away. Kathryn and Roy had a love affair that lasted 40 years. The last 20 years after Roy's death were hard on Kathryn. Roy had done everything for her. Even though she worked outside the home, she depended on him to make all

the decisions.   He was "the head of the family."
Loraine was thrilled and surprised when her Mom
decided to take driving lessons the year after Roy
died. She learned to balance her bank account and
kept herself out of debt. Loraine was so proud of her.

The years had taken their toll on Kathryn
mentally and physically. When she would forget to
turn off the stove, spill things in the floor and forget to
take her meds, Loraine and her siblings had her move
in with them. But now she was afraid of being alone.
The last few months Loraine could not even go to the
store for a few items.   Kathryn would become
hysterical before Loraine returned from shopping,
crying because she was afraid that Loraine wouldn't
come back. The last 3 years had been a drain on
Loraine and Billy's life and relationship. They couldn't
leave Kathryn to visit the children.

Therefore, she had missed many of the
milestones important to her grandchildren. She loved
Kathryn but she longed to be a part of her children's
lives. Now, Billy was sick and Loraine had no hope for
the future. She was taking one day at a time. As Billy
got sicker, she grew drained and felt out of control of
her life.

When she arrived home, Billy greeted her with
a hug and a forced smile. "How was your Mom?"

"She was Mom." That answer covered so many
questions and told him all he needed to know.

"So, it was a rough morning. I hate for you to go through that with her and then come home to me with my needs." His concern for her was evident and sweet. He had always been a sensitive husband. He knew when she needed space and when she needed his shoulder to lean on. She loved him for that.

"You are my primary concern right now," she said as she slid her arm through his. "Let's go get this doctor's visit over with, so we can have some 'us' time tonight."

Their marriage had been 30 years of ups and downs, but they always knew their bond would not be broken. As they entered their own senior years, they had a comfortable, secure relationship and a solid attraction for each other that helped carry them through the rough spots in the early years and seasoned as they matured.

Their three sons were married and happy with their lives. At least that's what appeared to be the case. Grandchildren brought joy to the entire family and each son loved his nieces and nephews as his own children. Get-togethers were fun and happy times. They were concerned about their father and wanted to help, but distance, jobs and children's needs made it difficult to give Loraine much relief. She understood, but longed for a day or two of "me" time. She couldn't remember when she had read a book, made a quilt or had lunch with "the girls".

Her philosophy was "You do what you have to do and don't worry about the rest." Good for a philosophy. Not easy to accomplish. She had God in her corner and He gave her the strength and comfort to make it through her days. Some day she would be in a better place, either in this world or in heaven. That knowledge was a great comfort to her.

"If we don't get a move on, we will be late." She opened the door and nudged Billy through it toward the car. The doctor's office was about 25 miles away. Traffic could be unpredictable at this time of day and Billy never liked to be late. They were quiet on the drive.

She pretended to look at the burst of colors of the trees lining the roads. She did love this time of year. Gold and red cascades of leaves floated from the sky dancing off the windshield and laying a quilt-like carpet on the ground. Today, she was not focusing on the beauty surrounding her. Today, she was silently worrying about Billy and what the doctor would say.

Billy was pretending to concentrate on the road and traffic. But he was also thinking about the doctor visit and how his and Loraine's life would change after surgery. This whole medical dilemma had come on so fast. He had always been healthy and strong. How could he have cancer and not know it? He was afraid of the cancer and what kind of outcome he would have with it. But he was equally afraid of becoming less of a man. He wanted to give Loraine a full man in their intimate times. He didn't want her to see him as weak.

3.

Peggy didn't have to wait long for Papa to get home. Some days she would hear him whistling as he walked toward the house. She loved to hear him whistle. She knew all was well with the world when Papa got home. He was her strength. She knew he favored her over the other children and she also knew that she used that favor to get her way with him when the others could not.

Tonight would be different. She wasn't sure how severely their relationship would change, but she knew it couldn't stay the way it had been. This was going to be a hard night for her. She dreaded it, but she also wanted it to be over

Henry whistled as he walked home. This had been a good day. All the plants had developed in the green houses to the point he knew they would be safe during the winter months. Winterizing plans were developed for the shrubs and grass around the mill. Mums and pansies were planted with pine straw bedding generously spread to protect them from any cold weather that might sneak in ahead of winter.

And to top it off Mr. Hightower had called him into the office, congratulated him on all his accomplishments and gave him a $.50 a week raise. After dinner, he might take Mama out for an ice cream cone. Things were looking up.

Henry always got a satisfied feeling when he turned the corner to their house. Humble as it was, it was dry, safe, large enough for all the kids to have bedrooms even though that meant two to a room, and provided by the mill rent free as part of his pay. So many men couldn't find work these days. Henry was doing fine by his family. He was proud.

He smelled the greens, cornbread and soup beans as he opened the door. As he kissed Mama on the cheek he said, "I know I'm a little early. Don't rush with dinner. I'll go wash up and find Frank. Maybe he will play a little on the piano for us. He has such a talent. I love to watch him playing. He does love his music, doesn't he?"

Mama offered a weak smile and turned back to the stove. "What a shame his night will be ruined. He's in such a good mood," she thought.

The chatter at dinner kept her mind off the inevitable, until Henry said, "Well kids. Your Papa has done such a good job beautifying the mill grounds that Mr. Hightower gave me a $.50 a week raise today. What do you think about that?" he smiled and slid his chair back from the table a little.

They all started talking at once; listing all the things they wanted to help him decide how to spend his extra money. "Hey, now. This money won't be spent on foolish things. We will give the first $.05 to the Lord and then we will save $.05 and the rest will go toward necessities."

Mama stood and announced, "Kathryn, it is your night to do the dishes. Choose two others to help you. Dad and I need to have a little talk with Peggy. We'll be in the yard. Everyone else, do your chores and finish your homework."

Papa looked at Mama in alarm, but he didn't say a word until they reached the back yard swing. "What's this about Mama?"

"I will let Peggy tell you," she choked out.

"No, Mama. Don't make me say it. I can't look at Papa and say it." Peggy fell to her knees in front of her mother. She grasped her mother's hands and laid her face on them. She was inconsolable.

Ola gently lifted Peggy's face. Tears were streaming down her cheeks and falling into Ola's lap. "This is the first brave thing you must do now that you are a woman. There will be many other hard choices for you in the future. Know that now. Get up, sit on the swing, face your Papa and tell him of your mistake."

Peggy knew Mama was right. She had to be strong for the next six months. There would be much heartache to endure. Little did she know the extent of the heartache and how many people would be affected?

"Papa," she began, but as she looked at his face the tears flowed again. "Papa, I am going to have a baby." The look on Henry's face broke her heart.

"How can that be, Peggy?"

"It only happened one time, Papa. Ted and I are in love and one night at the lake we went too far. I'm so ashamed, Papa. Ted loves me and we are going to get married. He is telling his family tonight. He will be over here tomorrow to talk it out with you." Words tumbled out of her mouth as if she were afraid to take a breath or she wouldn't be able to go on.

Henry did not speak again. He rose from the swing and walked toward the woods. Peggy watched as he disappeared in the shadows. Soon she and Mama heard an anguished sob echo in the trees.

"We'll talk tomorrow Peggy. Go to bed now."

"I love you Mama. I'm so sorry."

Kathryn wondered why Mama and Peggy had to talk with Papa alone. She was sensitive to every change in the family's routine. The time after dinner was saved for Mama and Papa to be together to talk about their day and visit alone. The kids never interrupted this time unless it was an emergency. As she washed the last pot she glanced out the window and saw Papa go into the woods. Then Mama came in to make sure everyone was completing their nightly tasks and getting ready for school the next day. Mama did not look Kathryn in the eyes when she thanked her for doing a good job with kitchen clean-up. Kathryn smiled at Ola but got no response

4.

Dr. Jones' office was filled with patients when Loraine and Billy arrived. They were told to sign in and take a seat. This was the third time Billy had been to the urologist. So, he was not surprised at the full waiting room. He signed his name and birthdate, grabbed Loraine's hand and they walked to a seat near the door that led to the interior offices.

The large waiting room was decorated in the latest interior decorator colors, with cool blues and browns. The chairs were comfortable enough if there was a long wait. TV's hung on walls in every direction to occupy patients' minds while they waited. It was not a happy place.

Billy was having a hard time sitting. He walked to the water fountain; took a sip; walked to the window; looked out; walked back to the sofa; sat; grabbed Loraine's hand; and then started the routine over again. Loraine tried to talk about the news, the weather, other patients in the room, but finally gave up and let him have his space.

It was more than 30 minutes before they were called back to the lab. Billy knew the routine, urine specimen, and blood work, then wait again. The first visit consisted of rectal exam, where Dr. Jones found an enlarged prostate, and a PSA test, where the number was high. The second visit entailed seven biopsies to determine if further diagnostic tests were needed. This visit was a review of the tests and details of options open to him.

The nurse ushered them into an exam room and told Billy to have a seat beside Loraine. Dr. Jones popped in the door with a thick file in his hand and a big smile on his face. "How are you today, Billy and Loraine? I know you are concerned about the results of the biopsies, so I will get right to it. First I'm going to tell you a little about why we took so many biopsies and what they tell us about your prostate."

Dr. Jones went into detail about each biopsy and how the numbers added up to complete a diagnosis for Billy. "You have a big decision to make, Billy. The numbers indicate that you have at least one cancerous growth encapsulated in your prostate. Three others are questionable. So, do you have cancer? Yes. What do you do about it?

"If you were 75 or older, I would recommend that you do nothing, because your numbers are not high enough to indicate an immediate danger to your health. And prostate cancer generally grows slowly. So, chances are you would die before cancer became a health risk.

"However, because you are only 62, there is a chance the growth could cause a problem later in your life. I'm going to give you some literature to read. You and your wife need to discuss what you read and make the decision that is best for you."

"These are your choices: 1.You can do nothing, take a wait and see position and we will watch it with PSA tests regularly. If the numbers continue to rise you can decide to do something at that time. 2. You can have it surgically removed. I would do the surgery. I would use a robotic arm to perform a laparoscopic procedure which means four small incisions to remove the prostate. And you would be done with it. Or, 3. You could have radiation of the prostate to kill the cancer. Sometimes this procedure does cause severe burns to the bladder, and if this procedure is done you could not have the prostate removed at a later date."

Billy and Loraine looked at each other with fear and questions in their eyes, but could say nothing.

"I know this is a lot to take in," Dr. Jones said. "Take the literature home, spend some time studying it, write down all your questions and come back in two weeks and we'll talk some more. In your case, there is no hurry. You do not need to rush your decision. This is a major decision for you and if you decide on surgery, it is a major surgery."

5.

Ola came back to the porch and waited in the swing until Henry returned from the woods. She did not go to him. She knew he wouldn't want her to see him cry. He sat beside her and took her hand. "What are we going to do Mama? She will be disgraced. How will she care for a baby?"

"Now, Papa let's just wait until Ted comes tomorrow. Hopefully he will have a plan. We can help them out for a while until they get on their feet."

"But money is already so tight for us. What about the other children? They are already doing without so much."

"We will be fine. We'll work something out. God will provide. He always does."

But Ted did not come the next day, or the day after. Peggy was hysterical. What is wrong? Where is he? She couldn't call him, because ladies did not call young men. He lived on the other side of the Village. So, there was little chance that she would run into him. She was thankful that it was the weekend because she could not have gone to her classes. The other siblings noticed that she was edgy and seemed to be crying a lot. But they did not question her.

Martha came home from her weekday job in Atlanta and knew right away that something dreadful had happened. The atmosphere in the house was subdued. There was no piano or horn playing in the parlor. Mama and Papa were nowhere to be found. There were no raucous sounds coming from her brothers' rooms.

She was 5 years older than Peggy and had always protected her from unpleasant situations. Martha was the one who walked Peggy to school when she started first grade. After a few weeks, she approached two girls who had tried to bully Peggy and threatened to go to the principal if they didn't stop. She didn't tell Mama. She just took care of things for her little sister. Peggy was petite with blonde curly hair and clear blue eyes. Many girls were jealous of her beauty and resented her moving to their town and getting all the attention from the boys. Even though Peggy was not conceited and didn't flaunt her beauty, her warm smile and good heart attracted the boys. She tried to befriend the classmates who were unpopular and wanted them to be accepted as valued people. These attempts infuriated the popular girls. Therefore, she had very few girlfriends.

Martha had been uneasy about Peggy and Ted's relationship. She thought they were getting too serious too soon. Peggy was just 17, in her last year of high school. She planned to go to business school when she graduated. She needed those skills in order to find a decent job.

Since Martha and Peggy shared a room on the weekends when she was home, she went immediately to their room and put her suitcase down. She found

Peggy lying on the bed crying. Peggy was such a happy girl. Everyone in the family gave in to her wants and wishes. She had a special way of treating others with such love and knowing what to say to make them feel good about themselves that they all wanted to please her. It could be interpreted as manipulative behavior, but no one thought of it that way. And Peggy didn't realize that her actions were getting her special favors. She was innocent in her motives.

Martha immediately went to Peggy. "Hey, what's wrong sweetie?"

Peggy rolled over and looked into Martha' eyes. "Oh Sis, you will be so disappointed in me. I've done something horrible. I'm going to have a baby." With that admission she burst into sobs and moans that broke Martha's heart.

Martha had to be careful what she said next. She did not want to condemn her younger sister. She knew how hard it was to avoid intimacy with someone you love. She and Charles had been dating for three years, were saving money to get married and had many nights when they came close to "going all the way" as it was called. It took determination and a pledge from both of them to wait until marriage to stop things from getting beyond where they wanted it to go.

"Have you told Ted?" She did not need to ask who the father is. She knew Peggy was in love with Ted and would never be intimate with another boy.

"Yes. He was concerned, but happy. He promised to come over two days ago and talk with Mama and Papa and tell them our plans, but I haven't heard from him. Sis, I'm so scared. What if he has changed his mind?"

"Don't be silly. He loves you. Anyone who sees you together can see that. His father probably has him doing some work at the mill today. That's all." Ted's dad was a foreman at the mill. Martha was hoping that he was distraught about his son's bad behavior and thinking about how to manage the arrangements. He had such high hopes for Ted.

Ted was quarterback on the football team. He was tall, dark, handsome and popular. He was valedictorian of his and Peggy's class and was currently waiting on acceptance to the University of Georgia on a football scholarship. He had worked the summer at the mill to save money in case the scholarship did not pan out. When he wasn't at work, he and Peggy were inseparable.

Friday night was left-overs dinner night because so many of the children were out with friends, at baseball or football games or on dates. Martha went down to the kitchen to start heating up something for her and Peggy to eat. As she entered the kitchen, Mama and Papa opened the screen door from the back porch. They looked at Martha and all began to cry. "She told you?"

"Yes. She said Ted was supposed to come over to talk with you. She is distraught. Has there been no sign of him?"

"No. We haven't seen or heard from him. You know how protective Ted's father is. Ted may be having a difficult time convincing his father to support their marriage."

The rest of the night passed with no sign of Ted. Martha wanted to go over to his house and confront him, but Mama, Papa and Peggy made her promise that she wouldn't.

6

Billy and Loraine decided on surgery. That way there would be no chance of cancer spreading, unless some cells had already spread outside the prostate. But the tests had given a reasonable assurance that it was contained within the prostate itself.

Kathryn needed to know. She would feel better about being moved to the assisted living home if she knew that Loraine would be spending all her time taking care of Billy and would not have the strength or time to do everything Kathryn needed for her day-to-day care. This would be a difficult conversation though because Kathryn loved Billy and would be afraid for him.

Fear was the one big weakness for Kathryn. She was afraid of everything. Always had been. She feared change as most elderly people do. But she was afraid of so much more. Since she was a little girl, she was afraid to walk into a room full of people by herself. She imagined that everyone was looking at her and judging her for her clothes, her hair, her walk, her mannerisms and anything else she could think of. She was afraid of being alone. She was afraid to try new technology. She was afraid of travel. She was afraid of making new friends.

And beyond fears, she was disinterested in everything except her children. She would not try crafts. She said she couldn't work jigsaw puzzles. She couldn't figure out word games. She had typed and used a Dictaphone on her job for 28 years, but she had no desire to use a computer.

She did love movies on television. And until her vision got so bad, she loved to read. But that pleasure had ended quickly with cataract surgery and glaucoma.

She doted on her children and listened attentively to every detail they shared about their lives. She was wise and generous and never offered advice unless asked, and then she was careful to assure her children that she knew they could make good decisions. She would remind them to pray about every decision and to follow God's lead.

Through her fears she was brave, accepted every change in her life and made the best of it, even if she would not have chosen that path on her own.

Loraine found her mother in the dining room having lunch. When she saw Loraine, Kathryn waved and smiled as if she were given a wonderful gift. Loraine saw that her mom was finished eating and asked if she would like to go out into the garden for a few minutes.

"Oh, yes. If you think it isn't too windy."

"It is a little windy, but you have your sweater and we can sit in the area next to the building. That should stop some of the breeze."

Loraine maneuvered the wheelchair easily through the crowded dining room and out the back door to the lanai. They positioned themselves well out of the way of the wind and direct sun.

"Mom, I need to tell you something."

Kathryn looked alarmed but gently asked, "What is it?"

"Billy has prostate cancer. We think we've caught it early, but we both want that horrible disease out of his body. So we've decided on surgery."

Tears flowed down Kathryn's cheeks. "Why can't that be me instead of Billy? He is still young and I'm an old lady. He shouldn't have to go through this."

"You've always taught me that we can't pick our challenges in life. We just need to trust God to help us through them."

"I know sweetheart. I just hurt for him."

"So do I Mom. But we're going to be okay. I wanted you to know about our situation so you would understand why we had to move you to an assisted living facility. I'll be in the hospital with Billy and when he does go home, he will need me to take care of him. I don't want you to be neglected. And you can't stay alone at our home while I'm in the hospital. We don't know what to expect after the surgery."

Kathryn didn't say anything, but tears told Loraine what she was thinking. "Mom, I love you and want you to be safe. This is just a situation we can't control."

"I know. But I'll miss you."

"I'll come to see you as often as I can and you will make new friends." In her heart Loraine knew that was unlikely, but she said the words for her benefit as much as for Kathryn's.

7.

Peggy stayed on her bed all weekend, crying, praying and refusing to eat. Martha was furious with Ted. She railed around the house calling him every name she could think of. Even the time she spent with Charles, she was inwardly fuming. Always honest with him, she knew she had to tell him the devastating news.

Charles took her in his arms as she began to cry. "Sweetheart, we'll figure something out. I'm heartbroken for Peggy. She is so naive and sweet. I know she is beyond comfort. But you need to be there for her."

"Oh, I fully support her. You know how hard I've struggled keeping our promise to avoid intimacy until we marry. I understand how it could happen with her and Ted. She loves him so much. I just can't understand how he can desert her now."

"I'll look him up and see if he says anything to me about it,"

"That would be so helpful. She made me and Mom and Dad promise that we would not contact him. But she didn't mention you."

It was Saturday night and Martha wasn't sure that Charles would be able to bump into Ted on Sunday. But she had confidence in his discretion. In bed, she lay awake listening to Peggy's sobs. She didn't sleep either.

Sunday, Peggy begged a headache and was excused from church. The rest of the family dressed and made the short three-block walk to The First Baptist Church. Frank played the piano accompaniment to Martha, Peggy, Susan and Kathryn as the praise and worship team each Sunday. It would be extremely noticeable if the family did not show up for the service. The three remaining girls could lead the singing without Peggy. Ola and Henry wanted everything to appear normal. None of the other children knew about the situation, so there was no chance for a slip-up. The choir director had chosen "Just As I Am" and "The Garden" for the Shelnutt girls to sing. Their harmony was smooth and strong. It was a sermon in itself.

The service went smoothly until Preacher King preached on the moral decay in the country with the introduction of swing music and the participation of the young folks in dancing. He decried that it would lead to the destruction of their morals and their very lives.

It was all Ola could do to hold back her tears. She and Henry had not allowed that kind of music in their home but she knew that all too soon everyone would know about Peggy and would judge them for being loose parents. They were known as the gathering place for the young folks because they all loved music. There was always singing, laughter and commotion at their house.

Sunday afternoons in the summer someone would haul out the ice cream churn, Frank would get his guitar and as the boys took turns churning ice cream, the neighbors would drift over. Someone would bring a watermelon and someone's mother would offer cookies and lemonade. Before the afternoon slipped into evening, the backyard would be covered in groups of children, teenagers and young adults sitting on blankets or in aluminum chairs around the long peeling painted table under the majestic oak tree, enjoying a few hours before the Monday routine.

Today there would be no ice cream in the back yard. Ola and Henry could hold their heads up in required social situations, but they were not prepared to deceive their friends about the trouble developing at their house.

When lunch was over, the boys decided to round up a group to play baseball at the high school field. Martha began packing for her trip back to Atlanta tonight. Susan picked up a book she was reading and curled up in the window seat in the parlor. Kathryn didn't want to be pinned up in the quiet house. She pulled on casual pants, strapped sandals on and headed out for a walk. She knew she would end up at the elementary school playground, but she always pretended that she was going on an adventure and could end up anywhere.

It was safe in Covington, but sometimes it was boring. At the playground she could sit in one of the swings and imagine living somewhere else. Her favorite fantasy was living in Atlanta. She had been born there, but the family moved so many times following jobs for her Papa that she didn't remember much about it. The Depression years were hard on everyone; jobs were so scarce and tentative that families never knew how long a job would last. Papa had been lucky to find jobs during this time. They had to make the best of it, wherever they lived. But the dream of Atlanta would always be in Kathryn's heart.

By the time she got to the playground there were already several children running around jumping from the swings and screaming toward the slide. She knew this would not be her retreat today. For a few minutes she strolled around the edges of the area enjoying the shade trees. There was one empty bench in the center of the crepe myrtle island. She loved crepe myrtles and started in that direction.

A slight breeze tickled her short dark hair across her nose. She brushed it back behind her ear thinking how much she hated her nose. "Pug nose" they called her. She knew she was not a beauty, but she didn't like to be singled out with a nickname like that. She had large dark brown eyes, a round face and a slight cleft chin

Some girls were awkward at 12 and 13 but blossomed by the age of 15 or 16. Kathryn still felt awkward at 15. She had some good qualities, she knew that. She had a beautiful voice; she was an accomplished clarinet and saxophone player; she had a quick wit and a keen sense of humor. But she tended to dwell on her perceived negative qualities. Everything seemed harder in this new town. In their former home in Smyrna she had friends, a school she loved and a church where she felt safe. She even had a boyfriend.

They walked home from school together. He carried her books and looked at her adoringly. They were too young to date, but he would come by the house several times a week and they would sit on the front porch and talk about their dreams. He wanted to be an architect. She wanted to be a mother and live in Atlanta.

Kathryn was comfortable with Hugh unlike any of her other friends. She was always on her guard with them. She compared her clothes and home to theirs. Hers always came up short. Hugh made her feel special. She missed him, but she knew they were not in love. She wasn't sure how love felt, but she knew it was different than her friendship with Hugh.

Kathryn's intuition told her that something was amiss at home. She could not put her finger on it, but it had to do with Peggy. She knew that as a fact, because Peggy had not gone to church. The family went to church every Sunday unless someone was sick. The doctor had not been called for Peggy, so it couldn't be anything serious physically with her. Kathryn envied Peggy's relationship with Ted. She wanted a boyfriend. She wanted to be part of sleepovers at friends' homes. She wanted a close friend that she could share her thoughts with, someone who was going through the things that happen to a girl at 15. Just when she began to get comfortable in a school and with a few girls, the family had to move. She hoped that this time she could stay in Covington long enough to make some really close friends.

Papa was let go from the mill when it became impossible for the bank to pay for a landscaper to maintain grounds at its three locations. Papa's salary had already been reduced by 40% and it was causing a hardship for him and Mama to even buy groceries for the nine of them. With the cost of groceries for their family, gasoline for Papa to drive to the three banks, tithe to the church, and pay rent there was precious little left for other necessities. He tried to look at the lay-off as a blessing in disguise. When the Covington Mill offered him a job at a 15 per cent raise, he knew that God had provided this job for him. There was no family discussion. They packed up and moved.

8

Loraine and Billy spent the weekend before his surgery quietly at home. There was not much conversation. Everything had already been said. They both had a peace about their decision and had asked God to lead them in the direction that fit His plan for their lives.

Billy was reflective. His thoughts led him back to his childhood growing up in Chicopee Village south of Gainesville, Georgia. It was an idyllic period in his life. There had never been another time in his 62 years that measured up to his memories of life in "the Village". That is how everyone who grew up there referred to the place. It was said with much reverence and followed with anecdotes of escapades, sports events, and hanging out in the woods which protected the back side of the houses from too much outside activity and securing the safety of the lake built as a reservoir for water to cool the huge equipment in the cotton mill. It was a life encapsulated within a 3-mile radius of the mill, the lifeblood of the community and the workplace of all its residents.

Everything needed was found in these 3 miles. There was a school, a clinic with a full-time nurse, a grocery store that would deliver groceries to the homes and put the charges on a "tab" for residents until pay day, a florist, a post office, a barber shop, a clubhouse, a swimming pool, a ball field, and a beautiful park.

The boys and girls who grew up in Chicopee remained close even after they moved away to other jobs and other lives. They continued to call themselves the "Chicopee boys and girls" and stayed in touch, cared about each other and were available for visiting each other in the hospital and mourning with families at funerals. No funeral visitation remained solemn for long when a group of Chicopee adult "boys and girls" arrived and began telling tales they remembered about growing up in "the best place possible to grow up". All the moms in the neighborhood were moms to all the kids and felt comfortable disciplining as well as feeding any child whose parents worked in the mill. They were one big family and respected each other because they all had the same values and beliefs.

There was a Baptist Church and a Methodist Church in the community and everyone attended one of these churches. The owners of the mill insisted on cleanliness and painted the houses each year, they even swept the paved streets and expected employees and residents to keep the houses neat and clean and the grass cut to perfection. Houses rented for $5 a month, sometimes for free if times were hard. If a child misbehaved or caused disruption in the community, school or in church parents could be asked to move out of the housing; sometimes they were fired.

Billy's life after graduation from high school and finding a job in Gainesville never lived up to those days. That is, until he met and married Loraine. He had been single for so many years that he didn't know if he could be happy settled down with one woman. Loraine and their children had helped him see that life could be wonderful somewhere other than Chicopee and in a more relaxed, peaceful manner.

He looked at Loraine and she caught his eye. Her smile made him believe that everything would be all right.

9.

Ola was cleaning up the kitchen, putting a few leftovers in the ice box, when the phone rang. The wall phone was in the kitchen, closest to her. She hated answering the phone. It was an interruption in their lives, but she knew it was a necessity in today's modern home. It did allow her to stay in touch with Martha during the week when she was at work in Atlanta.

She was proud of Martha. As the oldest child she had made good decisions, worked at the local drug store during high school and saved enough money (with a little help from Papa) to find a room at a girls boarding house and get a job at the Water Department for the City of Atlanta. She and Charles were saving for their wedding.

"Hello," she shouted up at the intrusion. Being only 4' 11" made it difficult for her to place her mouth close to the phone's mouthpiece. She could barely reach the hook to retrieve the earpiece. Her curly black hair fell across her shoulders as she tilted her head back.

"Mrs. Shelnutt, this is Charles. Can I come over now and talk with Martha, you and Mr. Shelnutt?"

"Of course, you are already a part of this family. You didn't need to call first."

"I just wanted to make sure you and Mr. Shelnutt were available."

"Henry is out in the garden. We will be available when you get here."

She quickly wiped off the table, dried her dripping hands on her apron and went upstairs to tell Martha that Charles was on his way over.

"He wanted to make sure that Papa and I would be available. I don't know what that's all about."

Martha averted her mother's eyes, closed her suitcase and ushered Ola out of the room. "Let's don't wake Peggy. We'll talk downstairs."

"I'm not sure it's good for Peggy to stay in bed. She needs to get up and freshen up. She will feel better if she eats something and bathes."

"Mom, there's time for that later. Let her sleep for now. Why don't we make some lemonade and wait for Charles outside at the picnic table?"

As they carried the tray with lemonade and four glasses to the backyard Charles came around the corner of the house. Martha's heart fluttered as it always did when she saw him. He came over and took the tray from her and placed it on the picnic table. Then he leaned down and kissed her on the forehead. Even though they were engaged, he was not comfortable kissing her like he wanted to in front of her parents. Henry saw Charles and immediately came over to the table.

He placed a basket of tomatoes on the table and said, "Charles, take some home to your mother when you leave. These are fresh picked and look red and juicy."

"Thanks, Mr. Shelnutt. Mom will love them. My family just doesn't have the green thumb that you have. Our garden seems to dry up just as the vegetables come in." He sat down in one of the aluminum round back chairs and tried to relax with his arms resting on the chair's arms. "I wanted to get over here as soon as I could today. I don't have good news for you. I saw Ted at church this morning. He was with Mr. Newman's daughter, Rosalie." He looked from Martha to Ola and Henry to acknowledge their surprise.

"What do you mean he was 'with' Mr. Newman's daughter?" Mother fell into a chair beside him and grabbed his arm.

"That's what I wondered about all during the service. I've never seen them together, I mean, like a couple. I caught Ted's eye as we left after the service. He excused himself from Rosalie long enough to catch up with me. He asked how Peggy was. I said 'How do you think she is? You deserted her.'

"No, I didn't. I mean, I did, but not because I wanted to."

"Looks like you had other 'wants' that took precedence over Peggy."

"Then he told me what happened. 'When I got home Friday evening after talking with Peggy, Mr. Newman and Rosalie were at my house waiting for me. They had been with my parents for a while. When I arrived I knew something was wrong. My Dad's face was flaming red and Mom had been crying. I asked what was wrong and then Mr. Newman showed me his shotgun. He said that Rosalie told him that I had raped her and gotten her pregnant and I was going to take responsibility for my actions. Of course, I denied it, because I've never been alone with Rosalie, much less intimate with her. But her dad would hear none of it. He said we were going to the Justice of the Peace in Monroe and get married. I told him that I wasn't getting married to her. I don't love her. I've never dated her. I have a football scholarship to the University of Georgia. I plan to be there in the fall. I don't know why Rosalie named me as the father, but it isn't true. He pointed the shotgun at me and said that 'it' was the truth and I was not going to take advantage of his daughter and then walk away."

"At that time, my Dad spoke up and said that I needed to do the right thing and own up to my responsibility. He wouldn't listen to my protests. He said Mr. Newman would use his influence with the athletic department at the university, talk with the coach and make arrangements for us to have an apartment near campus so that I could complete my studies and play football while we raised our child."

Charles finished his story by telling them that Mr. Newman had accompanied them to a Justice of the Peace and stood behind them with his shotgun while the vows were taken. When he finished talking there was complete silence among the group until they heard a cry of, "Oh God, no, no, no!" from the doorway. Peggy had come downstairs for a glass of water and saw the four of them sitting at the picnic table. Curious about their conversation, she walked to the door. She heard the last few sentences and fell to the floor.

10.

Loraine and Billy arrived at the surgery center at 5:30 a.m. to fill out paperwork and get Billy prepped for the procedure. The waiting room was partially lit as they sat down to wait for the call to go back to the pre-op room. Before they got situated, they sensed other folks entering the waiting room. It was their pastor Jim Hubbard and three deacons from their church.

It was such a blessing to have a church family that loved and supported you. All Baptist churches didn't function like that. When Loraine and her first husband got divorced, the Baptist church they had attended for years immediately cut her off from any support or connection. She was already hurting and needed the love of friends. Her idea of Christianity was that you love each other knowing that everyone sins and one sin is not more worthy of condemnation than another.

After a time, she found her way to a Presbyterian church and raised her 'tween boys in that church until she and Billy married. She found peace and love in that church and couldn't imagine ever going back to a Baptist church. But Billy was Baptist and wanted to return to his childhood church. What a difference this church made in their lives. There was such love, acceptance and support. She was happy in this church.

It had not always been this way. There were years when she prayed for Billy to accompany her to church. He always found a reason to stay home.

The three-hour surgery stretched into five hours. Hospital staff was sensitive enough to keep her informed about the progress. There were complications from the oversized prostate that had encompassed the bladder. Painstaking cuts were made to keep most of the nerves intact and to reconnect those that had to be cut to get the prostate out.

After the nurse notified them that everything was going well, Preacher Hubbard left to visit other church members in the hospital. The deacons stayed. Cindy and Russ came after they got the children off to school. Jeff H. flew in from California to be with his dad. Jeff L. came with his computer and worked as he sat near her.

Loraine felt the love and support of friends and family and was thankful to have children who made time for their parents and stayed involved in their lives when they were needed.

11.

Kathryn loved Sunday afternoons when everyone was home together. It was family time. They walked to church, helped lead the singing; when the preaching started they sat together. At home Papa prayed before lunch and then the room erupted with everyone trying to talk at the same time. There was a lot to catch up on. Martha always had a funny story to tell about life in Atlanta, either at work at the Water Department or at her rooming house with 10 other young women. The boys relayed mischief happening at school. Susan gave highlights of the latest book she was reading. Peggy would talk about Ted and where they were going after lunch. Papa would tell about the economy to keep them up-to-date on potential jobs when they finished school. Kathryn and Frank or Bill would find some off-hand comment to set them off laughing, when no one else could see the humor in it. Kathryn took it all in, not speaking, just enjoying every moment.

Today was different. Peggy didn't go to church and didn't come down for lunch. Somehow things seemed off, just not right. Kathryn decided to cut her walk short and go home to check on Peggy.

The walk home was not as beautiful as in their previous community. The land here was hilly and the workers' two-story mill houses were mostly surrounded by dirt with sparse grass, very few shrubs and no flowers. Even though the houses had large

43

front sitting porches, there was nothing about them that invited you to walk up the stairs and sit. Papa would change all that. He knew how to propagate flowers and flowering shrubs from seedlings. In no time, he would have this community looking lush and inviting.

As she turned the corner into the street of bosses' homes, things looked different. The brick homes were nestled in carpets of green grass. Azaleas, gladiolas and hydrangeas flanked the front of the houses. Forsythia bushes and crepe myrtles defined spaces between the large yards. Here and there some houses had daylilies, thrift and primroses as additional highlights. The sidewalks were lined with alternating crepe myrtles and dogwoods.

She was thankful that Papa's job allowed him to live on this street in the only wood house, but she felt sad that all the yards weren't as inviting.

She spotted Mama, Papa, Martha and Charles in the side yard. Just as she got to the corner of the house, they all jumped up and ran toward the back door. She followed them with her eyes and saw Peggy lying in the doorway. Her heart stopped. What was wrong? Peggy couldn't be that sick. The whole family was active and healthy. She broke into a run.

By the time she reached the door, Charles had Peggy in his arms and was carrying her up the stairs to her bedroom with Martha on his heels. Mama turned and stopped her. "Stay down here, Kitty.

Peggy will be fine. She just needs some rest. I'll come down and we'll talk in a little while."

Papa headed out the front door to the porch. Kathryn didn't know where to go. She knew Papa wouldn't tell her anything. He let Mama do all the important communication with the girls. He felt awkward with all that girl talk. He instructed the boys. He taught them to be kind, respectful, disciplined, good workers, God-fearing, patriotic and to respect women and girls.

Kathryn couldn't just sit down somewhere and wait for Mama. She found Susan in the parlor reading Emily Bronte's, *Jane Eyre*. Susan was always reading. She looked up as Kathryn plopped down on the sofa. "What's up little sis?" Susan was only one year older than Kathryn, but she acted as if she were much more worldly and intelligent. Kathryn knew that she wasn't as smart as Susan, but Susan's worldliness came from reading books, not from actually living out what she knew of the world.

Irritated, she said, "Didn't you hear the commotion going on in the kitchen and hallway? Peggy fell down and Charles carried her up to the bedroom to rest, whatever that means. Mama said she would talk to us later."

"Oh, Peggy, the drama-queen. Who knows what's going on with her? She is so caught-up with Ted she doesn't know who she is right now."

Time seemed to drag on and on. Kathryn sat and looked out the window, got up and walked around the room, walked to the kitchen looking for lemonade. Instead got water. Spotted the lemonade pitcher on the picnic table. Retrieved it and put it in the ice box. Went back to the parlor, sat and waited.

Finally, just when the sun was setting over the roof of the house next door, the boys trouped in-- pushing, shoving and laughing loudly. Papa followed them into the house, told them to wash up and go to the parlor. Supper had not been started. Everyone was hungry, except Kathryn. Her stomach was in knots. She was worried about Peggy.

Frank picked up his guitar and strummed a new tune he was writing. Everyone else sat quietly, somehow knowing that this family had changed forever.

12.

The three hour surgery turned into five. Loraine hadn't been concerned about Billy's safety because a nurse reported to her every hour. But she was exhausted from the strain of sitting so long with all of Billy's visitors.

Early in the afternoon her name was called over the call system for her to meet the doctor in a consult room. Only then did the deacons leave her with a thankful prayer for Billy.

She did not have time to settle in a chair before the doctor emerged from the two massive doors leading to the confines of the operating rooms.

He sat adjacent to her with a tired countenance and gave her the assuring smile she had grown accustomed to in their numerous visits to his office. "Billy is fine. The surgery took longer because I did not know how large the prostate was. It had wrapped around the bladder. It took some careful cuts to release it without damaging the bladder. But the outcome was clean and he should have no long-term problems with the bladder. Now, I've got one more surgery for the day. See the nurse at the information desk and she will tell you what room he is in. I think a stay overnight is all he will need. We just want to monitor his temperature for 12 hours before we release him."

"Thank you so much Dr. Jones."

"You're welcome. I'll see him in my office in three days. My office will call you to set that up. Rest and know that he is okay."

Loraine felt the weight of the world lifted from her shoulders. She claimed her overnight bag from the locker in the waiting room, got the room number from the desk and practically ran to the elevator.

She wanted to run to him to touch his face and see for herself that he was okay.

Billy was groggy when he was rolled into the room, but he smiled at her then closed his eyes and slept for two or three hours. Loraine tried to catch a nap, but it was not her habit to sleep during the day no matter how tired she was. She thanked God for bringing Billy through the surgery safely, picked up a book and began to read.

When he awoke, he smiled at her. She couldn't believe that he was so alert after being under anesthesia for so long. "How are you feeling honey? Do you have pain? I can't believe you are already awake."

Billy took her hand and said, "Boy, I'm glad to see you. I can't believe how long that surgery lasted. I know you're exhausted. Why don't you go home and rest a little while?"

"There's no way I'm leaving your side today or tonight. I'm fine now that I can see you. The doctor said the surgery was a little more complicated than he expected. Your prostate wrapped itself around your bladder and it took a lot of small incisions to get it removed. They were able to do it laparoscopically though. So you only have four small incisions."

"Well, I'm not sure what that means long-term, but I trust Dr. Jones."

Later in the day Loraine found time to call her Mom. She had to plan around the assisted living's breakfast and lunch routine because Kathryn would be out of her room for an hour each meal time. After breakfast there was stretching exercises in the activities room. So, Loraine decided to wait until after lunch when Kathryn would normally take a nap. She had to wait for the nursing assistant to bring Kathryn to the front desk phone.

Kathryn could barely hear on the phone, but she could tell that the news was good. Loraine promised to come see her in a day or two.

Billy was restless most of the night and it was difficult for Loraine to sleep in the recliner. Someone came into the room every hour to check Billy's blood pressure and take his temperature. If the noise of those interruptions hadn't kept them awake, the light that flooded the room each time the door opened would have. They both looked forward to morning, so they could go home and get some rest.

13.

It seemed like hours before Mama, Martha and Charles descended the stairs. Mama and Martha walked into the parlor with tired, sad faces. Charles went to the porch to bring Papa into the room.

Papa sat next to Mama on the couch, reached for her hand and patted it softly, never looking at her. If he saw the pain in her eyes he knew he would break down too. Martha sat stiff-backed on the piano stool. Charles did the talking.

"I know you are all worrying about Peggy. You're probably thinking that she and Ted broke up and that is why she is distraught. There's more to it than that. Peggy is going to have a baby."

The gasps and startled remarks made him stop a minute to let the idea sink in. Susan was the first to speak. "Well, they are in love. They can get married. I'm sure Ted's dad can get him a job at the mill."

Charles continued, "That was their plan. When Ted left Peggy Friday afternoon he went home to tell his parents. Peggy told your Mama and Papa. Ted planned to come over Saturday morning to talk with them and plan the wedding. However, when he got home, Mr. Newman and his daughter were at his house. Rosalie claimed she was pregnant and that Ted was the father. Mr. Newman had a shotgun and demanded Ted accompany them to the courthouse in Monroe to be married. Ted's dad was in agreement and would not listen to Ted's claims that he had never dated Rosalie or been alone with her and could not be the father of the baby. Ted's dad was so disappointed that Ted's future was ruined, football scholarships gone, bright future at the mill gone that he told Ted he must do the right thing and take responsibility for his actions."

Frank was beside himself, "That's not right. Ted was true to Peggy. Everyone knows how much he loves her. He would never have cheated on her. This is all wrong. What about Pegs?"

Papa spoke up now. "We aren't sure what she will want to do. She only has this year to finish before she graduates, but she can't go to school once she starts showing. Mama and I have to talk with her about going to live with my sister, Marion, up in Michigan until after the baby is born. But we aren't sure of anything now. We just needed you to know. Keep it quiet and love Peggy. She is hurting so much now. But with God's help we will get through this."

The guys drifted to the back yard to huddle and talk. Mama went to the kitchen to heat leftovers for anyone who might have an appetite for supper. Papa went to the greenhouse to work through his thoughts and do a little pruning. Susan put her book back on the shelf and slowly walked toward the stairs. Martha and Charles grabbed hands and went to the front porch. Kathryn sat for a moment letting it all sink in.

Tears began to flow from her eyes. She needed to see Peggy. She had a lot of questions, but now was not the time to ask them.

Supper time was quiet and solemn. Only the boys had appetites but even they ate little. Mama told everyone that Peggy was going to class the next day so that everything would look normal. The guys looked at each other with questioning eyes. Mama noticed but did not acknowledge it.

Kathryn groaned, "How can she do that? Everyone will look at her and call her names."

"Now Kathryn. No one will know unless one of us tells. She isn't showing yet. We need to keep up appearances until we decide what to do."

Kathryn wasn't sure about that, but she knew not to argue with Mama, especially now. She asked to be excused from the table, took her dishes to the kitchen and began to clean up. One by one the others brought their dishes in and soon the room was buzzing with questions about what was going to happen. Mama and Papa left the dining room and went out to the swing in the backyard as was their nightly ritual. The swing and the peacefulness of the yard at evening were the place and time that they were alone to talk.

"We're in a mess Mama."

"I know. I know Papa."

"How's that little princess going to face everyone tomorrow? She's so gentle and naive. She won't be able to look anyone in the eye. And what about the gossip about Ted. That will tear her up."

"She's a woman now. She has to learn to be strong. This is her first test." Mama sobbed into his shoulder.

14.

Loraine loaded Billy, his catheter and overnight bags into the car. She knew the next few weeks would be difficult for him and she prayed that he would be able to accept his short-term discomforts with a thankful attitude that now there was no cancer because the prostate was gone. Dr. Jones had said that there was only a slim chance that a cell had gotten outside of the prostate and had attached to some other part of his body.

They would keep a close watch over him for the next year to catch any unusual increase in PSA score. She knew they were blessed. They never really considered the other options available. She and Billy both knew they would constantly worry if the prostate had been left to radiation or a "wait and see" approach. No matter what changes their life would need to make, it was worth it to have the hateful cancer gone.

Billy collapsed into bed and fell asleep immediately. Loraine was glad that he would be able to rest while she prepared the house for their new routine. Those chores took longer than expected because the phone repeatedly interrupted her. Family, friends and church acquaintances called to check on him. Soon neighbors and friends began marking a trail to the front door carrying food. The stove and refrigerator were packed with enough food for a week.

When their close friends, Josh and Deborah, came by after work, they set the table and laid out the food so they could all enjoy dinner together. Billy could not eat much, but it was uplifting to see him make the effort to come to the table.

15.

Kathryn felt lost. There was no certainty in her life anymore. Everything she expected from her day-to-day experiences had become fuzzy. There was no blueprint for her to follow. What was expected of her now? When everyone found out about Peggy how would they treat her and the rest of the family?

She hurriedly dressed for school and went to Susan's door. "Are you ready to go downstairs?"

"I don't think I'll eat breakfast today. I might get sick if I do."

"Me either. How are we going to get out of this house without breakfast? You know how Mama is."

"I doubt that Mama will be concerned about our eating today. She has a bigger job ahead of her. She has to convince Peggy to get up and go just as if nothing has happened."

They made their way down the stairs and into the kitchen. There was no breakfast ready. "Mama we're going to grab an apple and head out. Do we need to wait for Peggy?" Susan tried to be casual.

"That's fine. Yes, wait for her. She should be down in a minute." Mama kept looking toward the stairs. In a few minutes Peggy slowly took one step at a time. When she reached the kitchen and saw Susan and Kathryn she broke down. "I'm so sorry to put you through this. I'm so ashamed."

Kathryn reached for Peggy with open arms. "We love you and will always be by your side. You won't go through this alone. Let's go together like we always do."

The walk to the school only took fifteen minutes. They reached the school a little before the doors opened. Other students were gathering around the steps from the street and leaning on the railings making small talk. As the threesome approached some groups stopped talking and looked their way. Immediately, Peggy knew they were talking about her and began to back away. With a sister on each side, she was forced to continue toward the front door.

One comment they heard as they reached the break in the stairs, "Poor Peggy. They were such a perfect couple. What will she do now that Ted has married someone else?"

Peggy almost collapsed when she heard those words. She realized that no one knew of her condition, but the word was already out about Ted and Rosalie getting married.

Kathryn and Susan walked with Peggy to her first class and stood around with her until the last minute so that she wouldn't have to make small talk with her classmates.

"We'll see you after class and walk with you to your next class."

"No. I'll be fine. People would wonder why you're walking me to class. Just go about your routine; try to act normal. Thank you though." She turned and went into class.

Kathryn and Susan almost ran to their first class of the day so they wouldn't be late.

Several days went by like this with no overt conversation about Ted or Rosalie. Peggy tried to get back into the fun but it seemed so trivial now. By Friday afternoon she had decided that she would not return to classes.

Kathryn listened for any mention of gossip about Peggy. There was none until Thursday, after Wednesday night prayer meeting. Evidently Ted's Dad felt he had to have an explanation for Ted's early exit from school. So, he told the deacons of the church that two girls, Rosalie and Peggy had claimed that Ted had gotten them pregnant. He said that Ted denied ever being with Peggy. So, he told him he needed to be a man and marry Rosalie to own up to his responsibility for the unborn child and to protect her reputation.

The deacons were disappointed in Ted and had hoped for him to be the first small-town athlete to win a scholarship and play for the University of Georgia Bulldogs football team. But they respected that he had indeed lived up to his responsibilities and would be a fine father and husband.

One of the deacons had gone home and told his wife about the conversation. One of his high school children overheard him and leaked the story the next morning. At first it was only a small group that heard about Peggy. But by Friday the story was gaining momentum in all classes. Kathryn overheard two of her classmates whispering about it before they saw her and stopped talking.

She was ashamed and embarrassed for Peggy, herself and her whole family. She left the class and went to the principal's office claiming a severe headache, which was not exactly untrue. She went home to share what she had heard.

Peggy was in her room where Mama was trying to console her again. Kathryn heard them talking but realized that they didn't know what they should do. The problem took care of itself by the time Papa got home.

He called the family together before dinner. The boys were late getting home because Bill and Ralph were trying out for the freshman baseball team. Frank had practice with the band as drum major. Earl had a job.

Mama had made chicken and dumplings, one of the family favorites. It was a dish that could stay warm on the stove. She took the cornbread out of the oven and let it sit on top of the stove to stay warm.

After all the boys washed up they gathered around the kitchen table where they had their weeknight meals. Papa held his blessing until after he had his say. "Well, we seem to have a major change in our living situation. Now, I don't have all the answers right now. But we'll work things out over the next two weeks. I've been let go from the mill. They have a virtue policy which I understand. Since our little Peggy is with child and does not have a father for the baby and as her husband, we cannot live or work here in the village. They had me sign a paper when I took the job that the Mill would not employ anyone who brought disgrace on the company or the village. Our situation fits that definition." Papa paused for a minute to catch himself, so he wouldn't show emotion. Everyone was stunned. For an eternity no one said a word, and then everyone talked and yelled at once.

Peggy left the table crying, "Oh what shame and disgrace and poverty I've brought on my family. I can't stand this."

16.

Papa looked at Mama warily. He knew he should have warned her about his message, but deep down he knew that he could not repeat the story to the family if he told her first. He should have gotten some advice from her about what they would tell the children so they could have a plan to comfort them. But his loss was too great to talk about with her alone. He was the head of the house. He should be able to comfort her with his own plan. He had no idea where they would go or how they would manage after the two weeks' reprieve were up.

Frank stood up and announced, "I can't help what has happened to Peggy or the rest of the family, but I intend to stay here and continue my music training. I have my own dreams. I'll ask Joe if I can stay with his family until I graduate. I can work at his Papa's store to earn my keep. I'm sure he will let me."

"Son, I'm not sure you can stay here and attend school, since I'm not employed by the Mill any longer."

"Well, I'll just find a way." Frank stormed out of the room. They heard the front screen door slam shut and he was gone.

Mama told the rest of the kids to clear the table, wash the dishes and clean up the kitchen while she and Papa had a discussion in the parlor. The kids knew something was upsetting their Mom, because she and Papa always went to the back yard after dinner for their alone time. Going to the parlor was entirely new. It must be bad.

"I know Ola, I should have talked with you first. I just couldn't keep this from the kids. They needed to know as soon as possible." He reached for her hand. But she pulled it away and turned from him.

"Maybe if you had talked with me, we could have had some answers for them. I don't know what they would be but you can't just dump this kind of news on kids and leave them to worry all night."

"I'll start looking for a job tomorrow. The Mill is going to pay me for all my vacation and give me a month's salary, plus what I've already earned this month. We'll have a little head start on the next job."

"If there is a next job," she said with anger and hurt. "Do you know how many men can't find work now? Why do you think you will be the one to be hired? And where will you look?" She began to tear up. Papa reached for her and encircled her with his long, strong arms.

"With God's help, we will get through this," he said.

There was a timid knock at the parlor door. Kathryn slowly opened the door and peeked around it when Papa said come in. "The dishes are all cleaned up and put away. Everyone has gone off somewhere. I just wanted to ask if I can skip school until we move. I would be so embarrassed to go to class with everyone talking about us. I wouldn't be able to concentrate anyway."

Papa and Mama spoke at the same time, "No, you may not skip school. We need to take good reports to the new school. You will attend class until the day we move."

"But Mama, I'll be humiliated. I can't face those girls."

"Yes, you can. You have done nothing wrong. You can hold your head up high and finish your assignments, attend class and act as if everything is normal." Mama used her firm voice. So, Kathryn knew there was no use in arguing.

The night dragged on slowly. Kathryn lay in bed unable to sleep. Worried about what tomorrow would bring. She heard the boys come in late and heard Papa's voice 'having a talk with them'. Everyone was on pins and needles. The next two weeks would be awful for everyone.

The next morning Kathryn was the first one down stairs for breakfast. Mama was making oatmeal with sugar and milk and browning last night's biscuits in a buttered frying pan. Kathryn put the syrup on the table after setting each place with spoons and napkins and pouring milk for the kids. Mama and Papa drank coffee.

Oh, how she wished that Martha were here today. Martha was lucky. She already had a place in Atlanta, and a job. She would not have to face the condemning faces in this little town. She and Charles would get married and have babies after the wedding, not before.

Susan was next to come into the kitchen. Her eyes were red from crying, but she tried to put on a happy face. Mama was serving the oatmeal into bowls and putting the biscuits on a platter. "Susan, go call your brothers down for breakfast."

"Yes, ma'am." Her voice sounded child-like and humble, unlike her usual assured tone. She tried to not let Mama see that she was upset.

Earl came next. He finished school last term and worked at a local packaging plant. He was eager to leave home but didn't earn enough money to support himself outside of the family. He contributed some of his pay to help pay the bills. He wasn't upset about leaving this job, but wondered how hard it would be to find another job in the town where his father might find work.

"Mom, I'll just take a couple of biscuits and eat as I walk to work. I don't want to be late." He really just wanted to get away from the house before the others came down. He didn't like confusion or conflict which the house would be filled with until they moved. His walk to work would give him time to think about what he might need to do in the next few weeks.

The two youngest boys, Ralph and Bill, didn't yet realize what a change their lives would take when they left Covington. They only thought about baseball and when and where they could play next. School was only a waste of time. But they knew their parents required them to finish high school before they could strike out on their own.

Mornings were always a rush. Today, everyone was glad for it.

17.

The next day, Loraine asked Billy if he was okay with her going to see her mom to update her on his surgery. She knew Kathryn was worrying about him and she did not have a phone in her room at the assisted living facility where she lived.

Billy said that he planned to sleep for several hours and with a phone by his bed and a catheter for relieving himself, he was set. Loraine was tired from her sleepless night, but knew she needed to go see her mom.

She maneuvered her Honda into the tight parking space in front of the assisted living facility. Instinctively she felt a tightening in her muscles. She did not want her mother to be here. This was the only choice she had for Kathryn's safety because she could not live alone and Loraine had to put Billy's health first right now. The last 3 years had been hard on Kathryn. When it was apparent she couldn't live alone, Loraine, Janice and Don had committed to having her live with them rotating every month, moving from one house to the next. That way each couple was keeping her for a month and then freed from that responsibility for two months. That had worked until Janice's husband got prostate cancer and was now bedridden. With Billy's diagnosis another decision had to be made. He needed her emotionally as well as physically and she wanted to be there for him.

A soft breeze caught her hair and blew it in her eyes. She shook her head to open her line of vision since she had her hands full of mom's supplies. As she walked toward the front porch of the building she was blinded by the golden beauty of two magnificent maple trees at the end of the parking lot. She stopped to inhale their beauty and said a silent prayer. "Dear Lord, help me be patient with Mom today. Is it my guilt of putting her here that makes me so impatient? She is trying so hard to accept this place and her new life. I'm proud of her. Please help me show her that and let her know that I love her."

There were several residents sitting in rockers on the porch wrapped in afghans or in jackets. It was a perfect porch-sitting day, but Kathryn was not out there. Once again, Loraine was disappointed that her mom was not trying to get involved with other residents. Her disappointment was short lived because as she walked through the automatic doors, she saw Kathryn coming out of the activity room with a big smile on her face. "I saw you from the window when we were exercising. I can't believe you're here! I'm so glad to see you!"

"Mom I was just here three days ago. You know Billy had his operation yesterday. I came to let you know that he is fine and resting at home. But I can't stay long. I need to get back to him."

"Oh, I wish you could stay all afternoon, but I understand. What is in those bags?"

"Just things I thought you probably need, like adult diapers, dental adhesive, toothpaste, mouthwash and some butterscotch candy." Loraine teased because she knew how much her mom loved butterscotch.

"Well, let's go to my room so you can put those things away."

"Mom, I want you to know that I'm so proud of you for exercising. It will make you feel better and have more energy."

"I try to come when I feel like it. I don't feel like it every day. It tires me out and sometimes I'm napping when the class starts. I've asked them to come get me, but they don't."

Loraine knew that this was the beginning of a long oration of how ignored by the staff that Kathryn felt. "Mom, you know they have a lot of residents here they have to look after. I'm sure they get busy and don't realize the time. They want you to take part in the activities."

"I know they are busy, but they seem to find time to help the other women. They even forget to come get me for meals. I've missed dinner two nights."

"Mom, that's why I bought you that big clock hanging on the wall right in front of your bed and chair, so you could see what time it is. And there is a schedule of all the meals on your dresser. You just need to look at it if you forget what time they serve meals." Loraine knew that this was the beginning of a recurring liturgy of complaints. She didn't want to deal with it today.

"Let me tell you about Billy. Then I have to go."

"You just got here."

"I know, but it is an hour drive down here and I need to get back to be sure Billy is okay. I'll come back in a day or two. You get your hair done tomorrow. That will keep you busy and tire you out. I'll come back Friday." Loraine put away the supplies as she explained the procedure Billy had and the lengthy surgery. She felt guilty for wanting to leave, but emotionally she couldn't watch her mom evolve into a pitiful state. Dear God, she had lost patience again.

18.

Kathryn and Susan avoided stares of the students as they entered the courtyard of the school. They had walked as slowly as possible, even stopping a block away and waiting until most students entered the building before they made their way to their rooms just before the tardy bell rang.

The entire day was torture for both girls. They couldn't concentrate on their lessons and kept their heads down pretending to read during classes. They met at strategic places between classes and during lunch so they wouldn't be able to hear what was being said.

As soon as the dismissal bell rang they met and almost ran home. How could they manage this façade for two weeks? They agreed they wouldn't tell Mama about the way they handled the day. She had enough to worry about.

The next day there was a group of girls blocking the stairs to the front door. As they approached, the group surrounded them and began chanting hateful, cruel things about Peggy and them. They tried to ignore the voices and push their way through, but the group wouldn't move. Someone yelled, "We don't want your white-trash kind in our school or neighborhood. Move out!" The whole group chimed in yelling, "move out, move out".

Hearing the commotion at the front door, the principal walked out on the steps and demanded, "What is going on here? Why aren't you girls in class? Get to your classes, now!" He corralled Kathryn and Susan in his arms and led them into his office.

Closing the door he said, "I've heard the rumors about Peggy. Are they true?"

The girls looked at each other, then back at Mr. Weintraub and nodded yes.

"I'm so sorry this has happened to you and your family. But you know the rules in this community. There is little room here for empathy or compassion. When will you move out?"

Susan answered through tears, "We have to leave in two weeks."

"May I make a suggestion?" He didn't wait for an answer. "This will be an impossible situation for you to endure. What if I agreed to let you finish your two weeks with home study? You will not be docked for days away from school and your records forwarded to your new school will show no discrepancy in credits and days attended."

Kathryn and Susan both answered, "That would be great Mr. Weintraub, but Mama would have to agree to it."

"I'll talk with her personally. I'll get your teachers to give me your assignments for the next two weeks and you can drop them off at my house when you complete them. We will miss your family. We've grown to love each of you during your short time here. We appreciate so much your contribution to the Baptist church and your participation here at school. I wish all of you the best. By the way, how is Peggy?"

"She's not good right now." Susan's answer was expected.

"Well, tell her that my family will be praying for her, and all of you."

The girls left Mr. Weintraub's office knowing that it would be hard to convince Mama that it was okay to be home at this time of day. By the time they entered the house, Mama was on the phone with him.

When she hung up, she grabbed the girls, sobbing inconsolably. Kathryn wondered how many more tears Mama would shed before life seemed good again.

Shortly, Ralph and Bill came home with a similar story from their principal. School would be held in the parlor each day until they moved.

Papa returned from the mill at lunch time with his personal tools loaded on a cart. The journey to their new home had begun.

19.

Papa was out all day each day making contacts for a new job. When he was at home he was on the phone calling friends in other towns to see if anyone knew of an opening for a landscaper, horticulturist or yard man. He would take anything. He had to secure a job so that the family had a place to live.

Mama spent the day packing up their meager household items. Evenings were quiet. No one had much to say since they spent the entire day together. Papa's prayers were repetitious pleas, "God show us where you want us to live. Provide a job and a place for us to live together as a family. Help me to know what it is I should be doing. Keep us safe and healthy through this time of trouble.   Lord, we trust you to provide for us. We love you and thank you for the life you have given us. Amen."

Everyone knew that the "safe and healthy" was directed at Peggy and the baby. One day Mama and Papa ushered the family to the parlor and told the kids to stay there until dinner. Kathryn, Frank and Susan could hear them on the telephone making long distance calls. Sometimes Mama would do the talking. They wondered why she was on the telephone when it was Papa who was looking for work. Besides, she hated talking on the phone because she was too short to reach the mouthpiece comfortably.

At dinner, they found out the answer. Peggy rarely came to the table for meals anymore, but tonight she came into the room with red-rimmed eyes and sat in her usual place. Before praying Papa said, "I have something to share with you. It is not a decision we wanted to make, but it is necessary for the family at this time. Peggy is going to live with Aunt Marion in Mount Clemens, Michigan until the baby is born." Gasps and sobs came from around the table. "As I said it is not what we want, but it will be better for Peggy and the baby to be away from the stress her situation has put on her. Aunt Marion has a spare bedroom and welcomes her with open arms. She will be well taken care of. After the baby is born she will return to live with us, wherever we may be. Mama and I will acknowledge the baby as our baby in the new town. Peggy will not be able to finish her last term of high school. After the baby is born she will take business classes to prepare her for a job. Peggy has agreed to this arrangement even though she is sad to leave us."

Peggy looked at her siblings with tears streaming down her face. "I will miss all of you. And again, I'm so sorry to put you through this." She left the table and they did not see her again until the next day when she, Papa and Mama left for the train station to put her on a train headed for Michigan.

Kathryn could not hug Peggy long enough or tight enough to last through the months she would be gone. Peggy had been Kathryn's best friend. Kathryn always looked to Peggy for advice and support. She wasn't sure how she could manage without her big sister around. Even though Susan was older than Kathryn, she had been the popular one and had lots of girlfriends to spend time with. She seemed bothered by Kathryn's insecurities and didn't know how to help her. Therefore, she was aloof and seemed uncaring. Kathryn felt totally alone.

20

Of all the hard times Ola and Henry had been through, this was the hardest thing they had ever done. Papa bought the one way ticket to Mount Clemens with some of his severance money. It was going to make the next few weeks and months even harder to manage financially but it was a necessary expense.

He looked at Peggy standing on the train platform with her one suitcase gripped with both hands in front of her. Her wavy blonde hair was pulled back in a knot at the nape of her neck, but it still sparkled in the sunshine. Blue eyes wet with tears looked frightened even though she stood straight-backed with feet slightly apart. She so wanted to be strong for her parents. She knew Aunt Marion and Uncle Chester wanted her to come and stay with them, but she did not know them. And she had never been out of Georgia. But she had brought all these changes on herself. She would try to be a good guest and help out all she could at the hotel.

Uncle Chester and Aunt Marion had moved to Mount Clemens thirty years ago for Uncle Chester to work with one of the major rose growers in the city. He, like Henry, had grown up in horticulture and loved working with roses. Since Mount Clemens had been known as the Rose Capital of the United States, it was the perfect place for him to hone his skills in growing roses under glass.

Uncle Chester also had suffered from severe arthritis for many years and wanted to take advantage of the mineral baths that had become a prosperous industry in Mount Clemens as a result of the unsuccessful attempts to develop salt wells. Mount Clemens had become world famous as a health spa and twenty-three major hotels and bath houses had been constructed. Aunt Marion had been fortunate to get a job in The Mattler European Hotel.

Ola instructed Peggy to learn everything she could from her relatives and to be polite and to work hard as long as she was able. She should look on this as an adventure and a way to see something of the world outside of Georgia. Ola wanted to grab Peggy and never let her go, but she was content with a kiss on her cheek and a quick, "I love you."

Henry could not contain himself. Tears flowed from his eyes. His princess was leaving and he would not see her during her pregnancy or delivery. He was so afraid that something would happen to her and he might never see her again. But he reluctantly gave her a final hug, kissed her on the cheek and said, "Remember, if you need anything, or if you're very unhappy, call home and I'll come get you. I'll get the money some way. As soon as we have a new phone, I'll call Marion and give her the number. In the meantime, we will call you once a week. You call us when you get there. Uncle Chester is going to meet you at the train station and take you to the hotel. Their house is not far from the hotel according to Marion. I love you, Princess."

"I love you both so much. I will miss all of you. But don't worry about me. I know where I'll be for the next seven months. I'm just so worried about you."

"We will be fine. God will watch over you and keep us safe too."

Peggy hurried up the steps and settled in a window seat so that she could wave goodbye as the train inched its way away from her life in Georgia.

21

Thomaston Cotton Mill in Griffin, Georgia, was expanding! Henry read the news in the Sunday paper. He knew what expansion meant, development of more buildings, building more houses for workers and landscaping all that property. He called to Ola, "Honey, come here. I need to get my suit pressed and a white shirt ironed. I'm going to Griffin tomorrow. I just read that the mill there is expanding and I want to get there before any other landscapers. They need me."

Ola rushed into the room and into his arms. "Henry, do you think there is a chance for a job there? It's so close to where we are now. The move would be fairly easy. Maybe our prayers have been answered."

Apparently the government's $150 million public works program was beginning to help the economy. Some men were going back to work. If the mill in Griffin was expanding and looking for someone to take care of its grounds, they must feel confident that things would get better. Ola said a prayer asking God to be with Henry during his interview and, if it was God's will, to put him in this job. They needed some good news.

By noontime the next day, Ola was getting anxious and could feel a migraine coming on. Even though the trip to Griffin was a mere 30 miles, she was not certain that the gasoline in the car could get Henry there and back. She looked in the pantry and pulled out the last bag of soup beans. These cooked with fat-back and served with cornbread would be enough to fill stomachs at dinner. Peggy's ticket to Michigan had put a strain on their remaining cash and they needed to have a cushion for moving expenses and setting up rent in a new place when they moved.

She washed the beans and put them in salt water to soak. Then she took the last of the fat-back and made slits in it so that all the flavor would cook evenly from the pork into the beans. It would take all afternoon to slowly cook the beans. Cornbread preparation would take place about an hour before she served dinner. The final addition to the meal would be spring onions and sliced tomatoes they had grown in the back yard.

The remaining children were in the parlor preparing their daily lessons as required by their schools. It was quiet in the house. There was no arguing or mischief between the boys. It seemed that the whole family had matured and become aware of the seriousness of their plight. In a way it was comforting for Ola to have her younger children in the house with her.

At the same time they all heard the old Ford rumble to a stop in front of the house. Before Papa could reach the door, everyone had crowded onto the front porch anxiously awaiting his report. By the look on his face they couldn't tell if he had good news.

"Let's go into the parlor and talk," he said as he grabbed Mama's hand. She looked into his eyes and knew by the twinkle she saw there that he had good news.

"Well, it looks like we will be moving to Griffin for me to take a job as the supervisor of the landscaping crew the mill has hired." Papa now allowed himself a big grin and a pat on Mama's leg. There was no immediate response from the kids. Henry looked at Ola in confusion.

"We're so proud of you, Papa." She said as she grabbed his hand. "This job will give us a new start in a new town where we can hold our heads up and be a part of the community. Thank you. We all know how hard it has been on you to give up this job here. But the new job seems much, much better."

After dinner when they were in their special place in the back yard Ola hoped to explain the children's reticence about rejoicing over his new job. "Henry, I know you were disappointed in the reaction of the children. But you need to think about how hard it is for young people to make changes in their schools and leave their friends. Even though this has turned into an embarrassing situation for us, it is still the home they had hoped would be ours for a long time."

"I know honey. It's hard on all of us. But we're so blessed that I was able to find a job so quickly. Do you know there were men interviewing that have been out of a job for six months? I don't know how they have survived that long."

While Ola and Henry were outside consoling each other and sharing feelings, the children were washing dishes and straightening up the kitchen. There was much concern about moving again and having to make new friends. Ralph and Bill weren't happy about the change but would just be entering high school and would have time to make friends before they graduated. Frank still held to his initial response and planned to stay put with his friend and finish the year in Covington.

Earl had said very little about the whole matter until tonight. "I think I'll stay in Covington too. I have a job paying me a decent salary and I don't know if I'll even be able to find a job in Griffin. Frank, you and I could room together. If you got a part-time job, we could afford a small place and remain here."

Frank was ecstatic, "Earl, are you serious? That would be great! Do you think Mama and Papa would let you do that?"

"Well, I'm almost 20 years old now. Many men my age are going into military service. I don't know why I can't stay here. Besides, that would be one less mouth to feed and if you stay with me that would be two fewer people to feed."

"Who is not going to get fed?" Papa spoke up as he and Ola came in the back door.

Earl looked straight at Papa. "I had wanted to have a private conversation with you about this, but since you heard part of it I'll just spill it. I've decided to stay in Covington where I have a good job. I can find a place to stay that is big enough for me and Frank. He can get a part time job to help with expenses and we can let him finish his high school here. It would be hard for him to start a new school when there are only a few months left in the school year." Earl folded a dish towel and placed it on the counter.

Kathryn was silently wishing Papa would not allow Frank to stay. He was her big brother. They were so close. They had the same sense of humor. He could always make her laugh when she was sad. He understood her. She would be lost without him.

Ola stared at her first born son with tears in her eyes. She realized that her children were growing up and had dreams they wanted to follow. She didn't want Earl and Frank to stay in Covington, but she knew they would be safe in this town. She had no idea what Griffin was like, or if any of them would be happy there.

Papa started to object and then closed his mouth and walked out of the room. "Let him think about this for a while," Mama **warned.** "He needs to sort this out in his mind before he talks about it with you."

22.

Earl and Frank contacted the owner of the boarding house and worked out a deal for both of them to share the bedroom at the rate for one. To compensate for the extra person at breakfast and dinner, Frank would maintain the yard and haul away the trash.

Papa was not happy with the arrangement but he realized that both boys were growing up and would leave home soon anyway. Earl began packing brown paper bags with their clothes while Frank helped Papa load the double bed frame, mattress and dresser into a truck borrowed from a next door neighbor. Mama pulled out four towels, wash cloths and one set of sheets, a blanket and two pillows for them to share in the double bed.

Their belongings were meager but they were excited to begin their new lives as independent men. Ola didn't have time to mourn this unexpected loss of her two oldest boys because she only had a few days to pack the remaining household items, clean the house and say her goodbye's to her closest friends here. Even though they were only moving a few miles away, she knew that there would be no contact with her friends after they moved. Life was too busy and gasoline was too expensive to waste travelling miles away unless it was a life threatening situation.

The family sat down for their last meal together on Wednesday night. Earl and Frank would spend the night in their new home tonight and Ola and Henry would move the rest of the family Friday and Saturday into their new home.

Papa began the meal with a prayer that had them all in tears. "Our Father, I want to thank You for Your mercy and grace. You have always provided for this family and guided our lives. These past few weeks have been the hardest weeks we have endured. We lost Peggy when she moved up north. Now, we will move on without our two oldest sons. Our family is being torn apart and I can't stop the fracture, but You have always protected us and loved us. I know these changes are Your will. Be with each member of this family and help us to remain close even though we will be apart. We love you. Amen"

There was little conversation during the meal. Each person was wondering what the next months would hold for them.

23.

"Mom, how are you doing today?" Loraine was concerned about the way her mom was sitting in her room with the drapes drawn and no lights on. It was an overcast day and the room was dark. The television, which was always on unless Kathryn was asleep, was off.

"Hey, darling. I was hoping you would come today. I've had a rough day."

"Are you sick?"

"No. These girls bathed me today and treated me rough. I told them to leave me alone and they said that they were the boss and I had to do what they wanted me to do."

"Mom, are you sure that's what they said?"

"Yes, they were so mean. I fought them. I know you told me that they might make me leave here if I didn't cooperate, but they don't need to treat me that way."

Loraine sat on the side of the bed in disbelief. Moving her mom into an assisted living facility had been the hardest thing she had ever done. She never thought she would have to make that decision. She and Billy had always said that they would take care of Kathryn until she died. God had other plans. Billy's cancer and treatment had changed their lives and forced decisions that they hated making.

She wanted Kathryn to be happy in her declining years and she had been so proud of the way her mom had handled the move. Kathryn cried at first when they told her that they didn't have another option to make sure she was safe and taken care of. But as Loraine took her shopping for new bedroom furniture, curtains and bedspread, she began to perk up and get excited about her new "home". The assisted living facility had a restaurant-style dining room, a snack area, an activities room where exercise classes were held as well as entertainment events, a beauty shop, large verandas with rocking chairs and manicured and landscaped grounds. There was a doctor on call, a nurse and medical techs on duty 24 hours a day.

Loraine knew Kathryn would be looked after and be provided with everything she needed each day from her medications hand delivered and administered, to help getting to the dining room for meals or to the activities room for events and weekly laundry service. She also knew that not every minimum wage employee was kind and loving. But most of the staff had a love of their jobs and worked hard to assure that the residents were happy living there.

"Mom, let's fix your hair and put on a fresh shirt. I'll open your blinds and let some light in. We can walk down the hall and see if they are serving ice cream yet. Would you like that?"

"Okay. I really need to walk. I'll feel better if we walk."

Loraine wished she had some appropriate advice to give her mom, the mom who always knew what to say to her to get her compliance as a teenager and to accept her life as an adult. She thought about the time in high school when she was dating a handsome young man who was very intelligent and serious minded. They had fun on dates, but there was a cloud that seemed to hang over his head. He wanted to accomplish so much with his life and he wanted to be sure nothing interfered with his ability to be in control at all times. He was one of the few teenagers she knew who lived with a single mom. He rarely saw his dad and resented him deeply, even though he never discussed this with Loraine. She became totally under his control, wanting to please him and be with him all the time. He was a good Christian and never did anything inappropriate to her. But she was definitely under his spell. Even though Roy never said anything to Loraine, he and Kathryn had noticed how mesmerized she was when they were together.

One night after she returned from a date with him, she was in bed reliving their evening when Kathryn came into the room. She was crying and knelt down next to the bed and told Loraine how worried she and Roy were about her relationship. She said that Loraine had distanced herself from the family and they wanted their daughter back. She kissed Loraine and hugged her and left the room.

Loraine could not get this episode out of her mind. Even though Kathryn never asked her if anything inappropriate was going on, she knew Kathryn was worried. Didn't Kathryn remember the warning she had given her years earlier when she gave her rules about dating. Kathryn had said that she and Roy could not always be there to be sure she was making good decisions, but God was always with her and would know and see everything she did. This statement had stayed with Loraine all her young life. She never wanted to defy this warning.

Loraine, Janice and Don attended Sunday school and church almost every week. They listened to a Baptist preacher who belted out "hell fire and damnation", and warned of all the evil in the world. He discouraged the teenagers in the church from attending dances, even the Junior-Senior Prom. Their community encompassed both the Baptist and Methodist churches, the elementary and high school, a library and an active business district with grocery stores, dress shops, drug stores, and a small shop that sold hamburgers, hot dogs, sandwiches, French fries and soft drinks. The Saturday hangout for teenagers in the neighborhood was next door to a small theater that showed Saturday movies for kids. It was an easy walk from most homes to this vibrant center or life.

A few blocks away Brownwood Park and Community Center was a favorite place to go and play tennis on one of the two courts or visit inside with a juke box and table tennis set ups. In the late 1950's and '60's life was laid-back and easy.

After Loraine got her driver's license, she was allowed to drive the family's extra car to school. To earn money for gasoline, she worked at the library three nights a week. During her senior year she picked up two of her close friends and took them to school each day. The heavy Mercury would only go 30 to 40 mph. The three girls laughed all the way to school that they could walk faster than the car would go. However, Kathryn was protective of Loraine's free time and was much more comfortable with her going out at night on a date, than driving to the Varsity drive-in restaurant in Atlanta with a carload of girls.

Kathryn brought Loraine back to reality when she said that she was ready to take a walk down the hallway to the ice cream parlor. Ice cream was being served and they enjoyed the rest of their visit eating the cold treat sitting next to a window where the sun bounced off azaleas and daylily blooms. The rest of the visit was pleasant and Loraine left feeling better about the situation, but carried an ever present guilt about leaving Kathryn alone.

24.

Moving day was clear and sunny. Surprisingly the furniture fit in the borrowed truck. Henry and Ola planned to make the trip again tomorrow after unloading the truck and return it to his next door neighbor, Hal. Then they would load the old Ford with the remaining boxes and clothes, clean the house and drive back to their new lives.

This whole move would be different from any they had experienced. The mill had no more homes in the community to move Henry and the family into. They found a six-room house nearby and offered it to Henry as a substitute. There was no question about whether they would take the home. They had nowhere else to go.

For Kathryn this was ideal. She would no longer feel subjected to the girls in the mill village. She would finish her 10th grade in the city school rather than the mill school. Susan would finish her last year of school in the city school too. Ralph and Bill would attend high school at the city school, never knowing the difference.

Kathryn and Susan were in the new house unpacking boxes when Henry and Ola got back from Covington. The girls would have to share a bedroom and the two boys would have to share a bedroom. But they were all accustomed to sharing.

The kitchen and the parlor were larger than in the last house, but there was no large porch on the front. The yard was level and there were several places Papa could place benches for the family to sit outside when the weather was pleasant. The closets were tight for two girls to share, but they didn't have many clothes anyway. They could make it work.

Beds were made, essentials were put away but there were still boxes stacked in every room. Martha came from Atlanta for the first time since the move. She jumped in and helped Ola unbox kitchen utensils. They both were delighted to find extra space after everything was organized in orderly fashion near the stove, sink and refrigerator.

At bedtime Martha was relegated to the parlor sofa since the house only had three bedrooms. She maintained her positive attitude and graciously spread a sheet over the worn fabric. She would be here only one night because she planned to go to Covington with Charles on Sunday. Plans for their wedding had been moved up since the unexpected move to Griffin for the rest of the family. She planned to catch the bus from Covington to Atlanta late Sunday afternoon. Just as she finished making her bed, Kathryn crept into the parlor to visit with her alone. She missed Martha's presence in her life. Martha's advice was always so thoughtful and assuring and it was always comforting to talk with her big sister.

Life was out of balance for all the family, including Earl and Frank. Martha planned to stop by their boarding house to see them before she returned to Atlanta. Kathryn and Susan had blended their personal items into their new bedroom easily and seemed accepting of their new living arrangement. Ever the second Mom, Martha wanted to be sure that her brothers had made a similar adjustment.

When she awoke on Sunday morning she smelled the familiar aroma of Mom's biscuits in the oven. The parlor was next to the kitchen, but Mom had closed the door to keep the noise from waking her. That was typical of Ola, always cognizant of everyone else's needs. Martha said a quick prayer of thanks for her loving mom.

The family planned to attend First Baptist Church in Griffin on their first Sunday in their new town. Martha didn't want to be part of that visit because she would not be moving her letter to the new church. She planned to marry Charles in Covington and set up house on the outskirts of that town. She knew it would be hard to face congregants in their church after her family's untimely departure, so she was going to the Methodist Church with Charles and his family.

She hugged everyone when Charles pulled up to the front door of the new house. He got out of the 1929 Ford and walked up to the door to escort his bride-to-be to the car. Always the gentleman, he also wanted to shake hands with Henry and offer his assistance in anything they might need. Martha felt a swell of pride in her fiancée's grace and kindness toward her family.

"I'll see you next Saturday, Mom. Susan and Kathryn I hope you have good luck at school Monday. And Papa I'm so proud of you. I hope your first week on the new job goes splendidly. I love you all."

As the young couple drove away, Ola ushered the remaining siblings into the house with instructions that they had exactly 30 minutes to get ready for church. They did not want to be late their first visit to the new church.

25.

Martha held Charles' arm as they entered his church. She expected stares and whispers but held her head high and smiled at familiar faces as they walked down the aisle to the bench where his family was sitting. Mrs. Patrick greeted Martha warmly and patted her arm as she slid in beside her future mother-in-law.

There were no unpleasant conversations after the sermon as she and Charles left to go check on Frank and Earl. The First Methodist Church was not unfamiliar to Martha because she had visited several times with Charles over the years, but she knew it would be an adjustment for her to accept this worship style so different from the Baptist church.

Today she was more concerned about how Frank and Earl had made it through the week than the sorting out of religious doctrines. She hoped they went to church but had a feeling they would skip it, feeling justified by the recent attitudes towards their family.

On the way from the church they passed the local park that had several basketball goals. There was a group of young men playing a pick-up game on one of the courts. In the midst of the crowd were Frank and Earl.

Charles stopped the car and Martha rolled down the window as he got out and approached the boys. When they saw Martha they ran toward her with welcoming smiles. She slid out of the car with hugs for each of them.

"How are things going for you?"

"We're doing fine. Frank attended classes and worked around the boarding house as promised. We're snug in our room, but we can make it work until he finishes school this year." Earl hung on to Martha a little longer than expected. Martha was glad they had come. She wanted to keep the connection with her brothers. Family was important to her.

"We're finalizing plans for our wedding. Soon I'll be moving back to Covington and commuting to work every day. I'll be an old married lady and you boys can come over to eat as often as you like."

Charles looked at her in surprise. "When we marry, you're not commuting to Atlanta every day. You will stay home and take care of our home and me."

Martha was surprised by his response. Even though they had never talked specifically about what she would do after they married, she thought they would need her salary to help pay bills, at least for a while. She said nothing, not wanting to cause friction between them in front of her brothers.

26.

Peggy was settling into her new home with Aunt Marion in Mount Clemens, Michigan, but she was lonely for her home and family. Guilt weighed her down with each step she took. She tried to be appreciative and help with the work in the bed and breakfast hotel, but a dark cloud followed her.

She tried to pray and ask forgiveness for her sin, but she was afraid that God would not want to look upon her in all her sin. Aunt Marion wanted Peggy to open up to her, but she knew she couldn't rush the process. There was time for conversation when Peggy learned that she could trust her aunt.

Tears for Ted had dried up after a few weeks. She didn't understand everything that had happened, and she still loved him, but she accepted the fact that he was married and could never be her husband or father to their child. She wasn't sure what she would do after the baby was born, but she couldn't plan that far away anyway. She tried to manage each day as a victory. She would worry about what she would do in five months.

She was in good physical condition thanks to her cheerleading workouts and routines. She was small in stature so she had to keep her weight down with this pregnancy.

Most days were a carbon copy of the day before. She dusted the guest rooms, folded clothes, towels and sheets, set the tables for each meal, swept the floors and supplied the bathrooms with necessary items. The work required little concentration, but kept her moving and busy. By dinnertime she was tired and soon after went to bed.

She wrote letters every other day to her Mama and Papa, hoping they would reply with some information about Ted. But their letters never mentioned him.

Her clothes were getting tight and uncomfortable. Aunt Marion offered to alter some of them to make her more comfortable. But soon she would need the concealment that maternity clothes offered. Mama and Papa sent her a few dollars each week and she earned a little money from her work in the hotel. She and Aunt Marion would need to take a shopping trip soon.

She missed all her family, but especially Martha. Their relationship had been the closest. Martha wrote every week, but it wasn't the same as having her to talk with. Long distance calls were so expensive that she couldn't ask Aunt Marion for that luxury.

Peggy was learning what it felt like to be an adult and responsible for yourself apart from your family. She wasn't sure she liked the feeling. She felt so alone.

27.

The hour-long drive home was made more irritating by the traffic building around the four o'clock drive time. Loraine had intended to be home before she had to deal with so much traffic. She was concerned that Billy had awakened and needed her, but realistically she knew he would have called her on her cell phone if that were the case. She tried not to relive the conversations with her mother, but that was impossible.

When she finally pulled into the garage at her house she let out a sigh and offered a silent prayer for God to give her patience with Billy and not take out her frustrations on him. He needed her love and gentle care. As she peeked in the darkened bedroom, he told her to come in. He needed some help with his catheter.

It was difficult for him to ask for her in this personal way, but he had no choice. There were some things that he simply could not do by himself. She could tell that he was in pain from the aggravating tube that tethered him to the urine bag, which was almost overflowing. Normally a strong man, the surgery had sapped his strength in a way neither of them had expected.

She wondered how long it would take him to get it back. He was embarrassed that he was unable to do everything for himself and kept apologizing for everything she did for him. She was thankful that he slept as much as he did. It would help him regain his strength and pass the hours.

28.

"Where is Susan? She said she was going to look for a summer job." Ola was beginning to panic. It was getting late in the afternoon and no one had seen Susan since early morning.

Ola went into Susan and Kathryn's room to double-check that Susan hadn't noiselessly gone up to her room for a nap before dinner. There was no sign of Susan. As she turned to go, Kathryn came up the stairs and entered the room to change clothes before helping with the evening meal.

"Kathryn have you seen Susan in the last three or four hours?"

"No, Mama. I've been walking around the neighborhood to get a feeling for our new home. Why?"

"No one has seen her. She left early this morning to look for a job, but she hasn't returned. This is not like her. I'm afraid she got lost or that something happened to her."

"Oh, Mama, don't worry. I'm sure she will return shortly." She said as she turned to grab a clean blouse from the closet. Her face paled as she looked back at Ola. "Mama, all of Susan's clothes are gone. There is nothing of hers in the closet."

Ola pushed passed Kathryn and began frantically looking for some item that belonged to

Susan. Then she opened the dresser, looking for undergarments or bed clothes. The drawer was empty.

"What is the meaning of this?"

"I don't know Mama. She was dressed in her Sunday clothes when she left this morning. I thought that was appropriate for job hunting. I didn't see her carrying anything except her purse."

Ola ran down the stairs and into Bill as she approached the kitchen door. "Have you seen Susan?"

Bill reached for an apple from the fruit bowl on the kitchen table. "Not since this morning. I saw her getting into a car a couple of blocks from here. She didn't see me. She was looking very intensely at a young man opening the door for her."

"Did she have something with her?"

"Yeah. She was carrying a pretty big bag."

"What time was that?"

"I guess it was about 9:30 or 10:00."

"Why didn't you tell someone, Bill?"

"I was headed to the baseball field. She didn't look like anything was wrong. She was smiling at the man."

"Do you know what kind of car it was?"

"From what I could tell, it looked like a black 1930 Ford."

Kathryn was crying, "Everything will be okay, won't it Mama?"

"I don't know Kathryn. I didn't know Susan knew anyone from this town. Wait a minute; didn't that Tom Brooks boy in Covington have a black Ford?"

Bill was quick to respond. "I think so Mama. But I didn't know they were dating."

"Me either, Bill. Did it look like him that you saw?"

"Could have been. He had his back to me, but his hair was blond just like Tom's."

Henry came through the back door. "Well, had a pretty good day...what's going on? Everyone looks worried?"

"Susan hasn't been home all day. Bill saw her getting into a black Ford about 9:30 this morning. Her clothes are all gone from her room."

"She'll show up. She's probably at the library, lost in her books."

"Then why are her clothes gone?"

"I don't know. You know how particular she is about how she looks. Maybe she took them to be remade somewhere."

"I don't think so, Henry. I don't think so. But I don't know what to do except wait for her to come home. If she willingly got into the car with someone, she must know him and I pray she is safe."

"Is there someone we can call?" Henry was looking for a quick answer to this new problem.

"Bill thinks that the boy may have been Tom Brooks from Covington."

"Why in the world would he come down here to pick Susan up?"

They all looked at each other with many questions in their minds.

"I'll call information and get a number for the Brooks family in Covington. We'll clear this up about Tom right now."

Henry lifted the receiver from the phone just as the back door opened. Susan and Tom Brooks walked in together holding hands.

"Mama, Papa..."

"Where have you been? Don't you know you had us all frantic not knowing where you were? You've never done anything like this before. What has gotten into you? And why are you with Tom?"

"Well, that's what I was going to tell you. Tom and I have been seeing each other at the library in Covington for several months. When we understood that our move would prevent those special hours for us, we realized that we are in love and didn't want to waste any time away from each other. So today Tom picked me up and we eloped."

"What?" Papa's face was red as he tried to control his emotions.

"Mr. Shelnutt, I know this is a surprise to you and your wife. But Susan and I love each other. We don't want to be apart a single day. I have a job and Susan is almost finished with Business School. She will make a fine employee for a company in Atlanta." Tom was interrupted by Ola.

"What do you mean a company in Atlanta? Susan will live here in Griffin with us."

"No, Mama. I'm a married woman now. I want to be with Tom. I was going to call you tonight and tell you that we are married, but I love you too much to tell you that way. We decided that we needed to face you and his family. We're going over to their house now to tell them. Then we will find a hotel room for the night and tomorrow we will go to Atlanta and look for a place to rent."

"Susan, you're too young to be married. You have so much life ahead of you." Ola tried to reason with her daughter

"Mama, I am almost 18. You were 14 when you and Papa married. You've lived your life. Marriage didn't prevent you from being happy."

"But we wanted so much more for you." Henry spoke softly. "Your mama and I have struggled over the years. We wanted to give you children so much more than we've been able to give."

"Papa, you gave us everything we needed. You gave us love. That's what I want with Tom." Susan reached over and kissed her Papa on the cheek and hugged Mama and Kathryn. "Kat, you have to finish school and be here for Mama and Papa along with Ralph and Bill. We will come see you each Sunday. We're still a family. Now, Tom and I are going to his family and tell them our good news. I love you all."

Susan turned, grabbed Tom's arm and practically dragged him out the door before she started crying. As they started down the walk to the car, Ralph came up toward the house. Susan squeezed his arm and continued walking with Tom.

Ralph turned and looked at them leaving, "What's up?"

29.

Kathryn put her books down on the kitchen table and immediately went into the living room to find Peggy and Dick. Peggy's return with the pink, dark-haired baby boy had added life and joy to the house.

Dick was asleep in the crib, the living room had turned into the bedroom for him and Peggy. There had been major adjustments to living arrangements and routines in the weeks since they came home from Michigan. But Kathryn didn't mind any of the commotion. Dick was so sweet and beautiful. She loved holding him and dreaming of the day she would become a mom.

She would do it a different way from Peggy though. She would have a wonderful husband who would take care of her and the baby. There would be no shame or embarrassment to that birth. Kathryn felt sorry for Peggy. She wished Peggy had a husband and father for Dick. Even though she knew Peggy loved Dick, she could see the sadness in her eyes when she thought no one was looking. Besides Dick looked just like his father. If they hadn't moved to Griffin the residents in Covington would know that Ted was the father just by looking at Dick.

Kathryn was not enjoying her studies at all. She was ready to get a job and move away from home, but she knew her father would never permit that, not until she was married.

Ola came into the room and the three of them enjoyed holding Dick and talking baby-talk to him. Ola and Henry had never wavered in their support of Peggy. They introduced Dick as their child and held their heads high as neighbors looked at them with disdain for having a baby at their ages.

Henry had been concerned about the tight quarters at home since Peggy returned. He felt that she and Dick needed some space of their own. It just wasn't right for them to sleep in the living room. He asked his boss if he could get additional pay equivalent to the gratis for the home they were in, so that he could find a larger house. As it turned out, the company needed the home for a new manager they were moving from Atlanta to Griffin. It was a new position and they had not previously had a need for housing for that job.

At the dinner table Henry told the family about the need to move and the extra pay he would receive for living outside company housing. "I need you, Ola and the girls, to begin the search for a new place large enough for all of us to have some privacy."

"That means we will have to move again." Bill and Ralph were not happy about the additional work.

"That's right. And all that lifting and hauling will build strong arms to make you better at baseball." Henry winked at Ola.

"As a matter of fact, Pop, there is something Bill and I wanted to talk with you about," Ralph leaned over his plate and looked at Henry. He used the pet phrase "Pop" when he wanted to sound confident and relaxed about what he was about to ask Papa. "Bill and I saw a posting on the message board at school for afterschool work for strong, energetic boys to help at a mattress factory about three blocks from here. Bill and I could go there after school and earn some money to help with the bills and put some back for us to buy a car. Playing baseball is for kids and we're getting too old to do that stuff all the time. We can play on Sunday's after church, if we want."

"Hold on now. I don't want you to think you can get this job and use it as an excuse to quit school."

"That's not what we would do, Pop. We would like to help...it's our duty to help, with bill paying. And it wouldn't hurt to have a little spending money in our pockets."

"Well, I guess it won't hurt for you to go check this out and see if you can do it after school."

Ralph looked at Bill with his victory smile and they left the table to discuss their plans to apply for the job.

"Mom, it looks like all of our children are growing up. Not sure I like that so much." Henry slid his chair back from the table and took his dishes to the sink. "I'll meet you in the yard in a few minutes."

As it turned out, when Ralph and Bill went for their interview the next day they saw a "For Rent" sign on a house one block from the mattress factory. They reported that to Ola and Henry at dinner and told them they had both gotten jobs. The factory was a small family business and their jobs would consist of moving the mattresses out of the production area, wrap them in shipping paper and stack them by date in the inventory room.

The next day, Ola took Peggy to look at the house that was for rent. The tree-lined street was occupied with white clapboard homes on level lots. They were not large houses, but were inviting and cozy. There were some shrubs and thrift for landscaping and plenty of room to add other small plants to brighten the front lawn. The sign on the front door indicated that the owner lived next door. Ola and Peggy walked over and before they could knock were greeted by an elderly woman with grey hair pulled into a bun at the nape of her neck.

She smiled and asked if they wanted to look at the house next door. She said she had had several families look at the house, but it was too large for most of them and too expensive for the others.

Ola was afraid that the rent would be too much for them too, but she wanted to see it anyway. The house was well-kept and spacious on the inside. There was a nice large kitchen with an eating area, no dining room but a good sized living room and four bedrooms. It was perfect for their family with Ralph and Bill sharing a room and Dick in the room with Peggy. That allowed Kathryn to have her own room and Ola and Henry to have some needed privacy.

Papa had told Ola that the rent could go up to $50 a month. They would only need an additional $10 month plus his $40 housing expense to make the payments. Ralph and Bill would chip in $2/week each to make up more than the additional $10.

Ola gladly gave Mrs. Pressley $10 to hold the home until they could move in the next week.

30

For Kathryn the new house seemed much larger than any place they had ever lived. It was one-story and spread out over the yard in a manner that each bedroom had a beautiful view of the back yard. The kitchen ran the width of the house with the entrance and living room across the front.

Peggy was comfortable in the new surroundings. Dick was growing so fast and needed her constant attention less and less. She was getting restless. "Mama, do you think that if I could find a job in a restaurant or cafeteria counter at the drug store, you could keep an eye on Dick while I work? I need to do something to get out and be with people. I'm going crazy staying inside every day. Besides, I need to start paying my share of living expenses."

"I don't see that as a problem. He is such a sweet boy and I love him so much. If you are sure that's what you want to do, I'm fine with it."

"Thank you so much, Mama. I appreciate so much all that you and Papa have done for me. I know I've cost you much of your savings. I hope I can pay you back for all you've given me and Dick. I'll go tomorrow and look for a job."

The lunch counter at the local drug store was in need of a waitress. Peggy's perky persona and soft beauty made her the perfect candidate. The fact that she hadn't graduated from high school worked in her favor, because the store's owner thought she would stay with the job longer if she had less chance of finding a better job.

Being with people every day brought back her natural good nature and enthusiasm for life. She loved joking with the men who came there to grab a quick lunch every day and she and the other waitress became good friends.

Kathryn would stop by some days after school and Peggy would serve her a coke or lemonade. They resumed their close sister relationship that Kathryn had missed so much. But the routine of school and lack of direction for what she would do after graduating made Kathryn antsy to get on with her life too.

As Peggy began to date, she introduced Kathryn to boys who could be potential boyfriends for her. But Kathryn wasn't interested in any of them. She had already decided that as the school year ended she would move to Atlanta, go to business school and live in a boarding house like Martha.

A certain young man came into the diner every day around four o'clock. He always ordered coffee and sat there for an hour or so making small talk with Peggy. She enjoyed his quick wit and his dark hair and muscular build held her attention. Eventually he asked her out. At first she was hesitant. The thought of Ted and the hurt he had caused her were still raw to her spirit. But Bud was patient and continued to visit her every day. He asked if he could drive her home, but she was uneasy with the thought of getting in the car with someone she didn't know very well.

She decided she would ask Mary, the other waitress, if she knew anything about Bud or his family. "I went to school with his sister and even went to spend the night at their house several times when we were in grade school. They are a fine, working-class family. As you have seen, Bud always has grease under his fingernails. He works as a mechanic. And he is a good one. He's the backbone of the business where he works."

That endorsement made Peggy feel better. So, the next time Bud mentioned them going to a movie, Peggy said yes. From that night on they were together several nights a week. Eventually, Peggy knew she had to tell Bud the truth about Dick. Even though he called Ola Mama, Peggy felt she was being dishonest with Bud for not telling him that Dick was her son.

After they had been seeing each other for about a month, Peggy asked Bud to take her home one afternoon. As they pulled up to the curb she said, "Bud there is something I want to tell you. I know we haven't known each other long, but this is something you need to know if we are going to continue seeing each other."

"Okay. I'm all ears." He turned to face her in the car and leaned back against the door.

"I've enjoyed our time together and I would like to continue seeing you."

"Me too."

"Well, you may change your mind...and I'll understand if you do...once I tell you about me."

"Oh, I don't think so. I'm getting very fond of you and your family."

"They think the world of you. But this is about me. Dick is not my brother. He is my son. I was madly in love with his father and we planned to marry. But he was trapped into marrying another woman. Therefore, Mama and Papa sent me to Michigan to have Dick at my aunt's home. We returned home and Mama and Papa told everyone that Dick is their unexpected baby. They did that to protect me and save me embarrassment and shame. But I still feel shame. Shame that I was so weak to give in to that man/boy before we were married. I love Dick and I would never be with anyone who couldn't accept him." The words poured out of her mouth without pausing. She was afraid she wouldn't be able to finish if she stopped.

Bud took her hand, looked into those blue eyes and said, "You are a beautiful woman, inside and out. I'm in love with you and I already love Dick, whether he is your brother or son. I want to spend the rest of my life with you and if Dick gets to come in the bargain, that's even better."

Peggy's tears were unstoppable. She squeezed Bud's hand until he took her in his arms and kissed her. "That was a poor proposal, but would you consider it?" He said as he wiped her tears away.

31.

Kathryn was happy for Peggy. She felt that Bud would take care of Peggy and Dick. He was a gentle, soft-spoken man. He had a dirty job but it was honest work and he was respected for his skill, integrity and dedication to his customers. He would be a good father for Dick. The family had never blamed Peggy for disrupting their former life. They felt love and concern for her. She never faced animosity for her failure, but she always carried her shame for what she had caused. Dick was loved as a gift from God for the joy he brought to the family. No one resented him or the attention he got from Papa and Ola.

But when Kathryn looked at her plight, there was no one there to support her and understand her feelings of being an outsider and embarrassment about her sister's choices. She felt like everyone looked at her family as trash. She could see judgment in the eyes of the women at church. There was nowhere she could feel safe and valuable like she had just a couple of years before. She constantly looked down when she met other people on the street.

At school she never raised her hand to answer a question the teacher asked. She ate lunch by herself and walked to school and home by herself. She had no joy in her life. Her usual dry sense of humor had disappeared. Her love of music was gone. She no longer practiced her clarinet or saxophone. No one else in the home played music. Her main goal was to get through the day and rush home to the quiet and solitude her home provided.

Laughter had left their home. There was no chatter at the dinner table. Ralph and Bill were exhausted after a day of classes and four hours at the mattress factory. After dinner dishes were done everyone went to their rooms until the next morning.

Once a month, Earl and Frank drove over from Covington for Sunday dinner. That was the highlight of a dreary life for Kathryn. Martha and Charles only came occasionally. Frank would sit at the piano and play some new song he had heard and tell tall tales about its origin. Even, serious Earl would smile at Frank's antics.

On one particular Sunday afternoon, Earl was especially solemn. Frank did not offer to play any songs to entertain the reduced family. Kathryn had learned to recognize when something was up. When the dishes were done and they retired to the living room, Dick ran through the open door and hugged Ola. Peggy and Bud were right behind him.

They had settled into Bud's small apartment after their private marriage ceremony. Things seemed good for them. As they took their seat with the group, Earl cleared his throat and everyone looked his way.

"Well, I have some news to share with you today. I have been offered an opportunity to understudy with a large insurance company. Seems

118

my math skills make me a good candidate for this training. If I succeed with the classes, I'll be offered a position in the Atlanta office as an underwriter. It is an opportunity I never expected to have. The only issue is Frank."

"What do you mean that Frank is an issue?" Papa leaned forward in his chair.

"Well, I must train in Atlanta, so they will set me up in a boarding house there during my training. Therefore, Frank won't have me as a roommate to share expenses. I don't think he can afford to keep the room in Covington by himself."

"We're so excited for you Earl. You must take this opportunity. We will figure out something for Frank. When will you start this training?"

"They have given me two weeks to work a notice at my job. So, I'll be leaving after that. I'll drive down the weekend after my two weeks are up."

Everyone gathered around Earl to hug and congratulate him. Frank beamed with pride for his older brother. He had no concern for himself. His positive attitude and good nature would not allow him to worry about himself. He knew God would offer something for him. What could have been a stressful afternoon turned into a celebration for Earl.

At the end of two weeks, Earl and Frank came by the house unexpectedly. When the car pulled in front of the house, Kathryn looked out the front window and saw Earl getting out of the car with a slender male in an army uniform. She wondered who that could be and called Ola and Henry to come into the room. Suddenly she realized that it was Frank with Earl. What was he doing in an army uniform?

The door opened and Frank danced into the room, his face wore a huge smile and arms outstretched. "Hey Pop, meet your first army recruit from the family."

"What do you mean, Frank? You're too young to volunteer for the army. What were you thinking? Things are getting serious now. We may be going to war."

"I know Pop. But I have no skills. No job to pay enough to keep me in an apartment or boarding house. The army will feed me, house me and send me to wonderful places AND pay me for it. What a deal!"

Henry had no answer for that. If war was imminent, all the boys could get drafted anyway. At least Frank could get training during peace time. The only response was, "I'm proud of you son."

"I'm dropping him off at Fort McPherson on my way to Atlanta. I'll make sure he gets to the right place." Earl wanted to be seen as the older son who could take care of his siblings.

That night Kathryn lay in bed feeling torn. Her whole family was disintegrating. She had no prospects of anything positive in her life. She hated school. She was lonely and miserable.

32.

The Sunday meal was loud and rowdy like old times at the Shelnutt house. Everyone had so much to share about their lives that it felt like old times even though this was the good-bye lunch for Frank. He was headed to boot camp in North Carolina. Kathryn reveled in the energy.

When Martha and Charles arrived they were bombarded with all the news. But they had some news of their own. "Everyone, we're planning a spring wedding. We would like to marry here in the backyard if that's okay with everyone. I'm saving money like crazy so we will be able to afford a nice home in Covington." Martha paused to get reactions from everyone. There was a long silence.

Finally Papa hugged her and shook Charles' hand. "A young couple should live where they choose. We would love for you to marry here."

"It just seems like a place where we all are getting a fresh start. And I know you will be able to make the backyard beautiful by then, Papa."

"Looks like we've got a lot to look forward to then." Papa reached for Ola and smiled his knowing smile at her. He knew she was fighting back tears. The family was changing too much, too fast for both of them.

Charles and Papa drifted out to the back yard to smoke as Frank moved toward the piano. He picked a few songs out on the keyboard and then motioned to Martha. "Come over with Peggy and Kitty. It's been a long time since you have blessed us with your harmony. We need to hear my sisters sing."

The three sisters, wrapped arms around each other's waists and began an a cappella version of "Boogie Woogie Bugle Boy".

For the next half hour they sang and rejoiced in being together as a family. Frank backed them up with piano after a time and the whole family joined together singing, a solidifying exercise for them all.

The whole experience took Kathryn back to happy times. She wanted that. She wanted to feel part of her family. She wanted to have a family of her own. She wanted to be away from school and out in the world, making her own way. She wanted to be taken care of and belong. She thought she was a long way from any of that happening.

As she was leaving, Martha told Peggy and Kathryn they needed to practice each weekend when she came home. Her company was having a talent contest and awarding $100 to the winner. Peggy and Kathryn both were eager to participate and agreed to be available every Sunday afternoon for three hours to practice.

Kathryn was more than eager. It gave her something to look forward to. She could go through the motions at school just to get to the weekend. The contest was two months away, but the three had sung together all their lives so the only reason they needed to practice was to find the best arrangement.

33

Christmas came and went without much celebration at the Shelnutt house. Frank had been sent to Germany after boot camp. Martha and Charles came down for the afternoon but seemed to be struggling with private issues. Earl was late for the noon meal, which was not like him at all.

The highlight of the day was watching Dick enjoying the few toys Santa had brought him. Papa had built him a wooden train set and Peggy and Bud had scraped together enough money to buy a used tricycle which Bud cleaned and painted. Kathryn baked sugar cookies and decorated them with red and green sugar crystals.

Ralph and Bill had saved enough money from their job at the mattress factory to buy Dick a baseball and glove. Martha bought him a red sweater and practical Earl presented Peggy and Bud with a life insurance policy. Ola crocheted gloves and a sock cap to keep him warm.

Since Frank was not there to play the piano after lunch, Martha, Peggy and Kathryn sang their favorite Christmas songs, starting with *White Christmas* and ending with *Oh Holy Night*.

Sitting in the living room with the Christmas tree casting a glow over everyone made Kathryn thankful that she had such a loving family. They had faced several difficult years but still supported each other and came together in love and respect for their parents. After the singing was over it seemed that no one wanted to be the first to end their time together. Maybe they all knew that this might be the last time they would come together as a family.

Eventually, Earl cleared his throat and leaned forward in his familiar way of getting attention. "Mom, Pop, everyone. I've met someone that I'm very fond of. I want to bring her home to meet you. She couldn't come today because she does not share our Christian beliefs. But she is a good woman and a solid friend to me."

Ola looked to Henry. She wanted to question Earl's thinking about this relationship. She wanted to yell at him to go slow with this woman. She could see a definite split in their family because of her beliefs, or lack thereof.

Henry looked at his oldest son. The quiet, introverted, purposeful, intelligent man he had become. He was proud of the choices he had made up until this time. He had to trust that Earl had thought things through and knew what he was doing. But love does cloud one's thinking.

"Of course, son. Bring her to meet us. I'm sure she is a lovely woman."

Earl's face lit up and he leapt to his feet. "Thank you Pop. I know you all will love Muriel. She is sweet and kind and beautiful to me."

He walked quickly to the door. "I'll bring her next weekend. Thank you."

Ola looked at Henry. "How could you be so ingratiating. I think Earl is making a big mistake. He has never had a girlfriend. He is mistaking her kindness for something more. She may be using him. Or maybe she is in trouble and is taking advantage. How can we allow a non-Christian into our home?"

"Hold on Sweetheart. I'm not blessing their marriage or anything like that. I am just allowing our son to bring a friend home to meet us. Aren't we all covered by God's love, even the unbelieving?"

"Well, I don't want her to unduly influence him in his faith."

"He is a grown man. This is between him and God."

Martha rose to change the subject. "Okay sisters. We need to practice. We only have two more weekends before the competition."

34

The weeks since Billy's surgery had been difficult for him. The catheter had limited his ability to move about freely and therefore his energy level was still low. One highlight of his days was calls he received from his friends.

Loraine was grateful for these calls. They took his mind off his condition for a little while. One afternoon three of his best friends appeared at the door with doughnuts and chocolate layer cake, two of his favorite sweets. Loraine made a fresh pot of coffee and set them up in the office to visit.

Immediately she could hear laughter coming from Billy as well as the other men. Over the course of a couple of hours as she worked in the kitchen she could hear stories of their escapades when they were young. They all grew up in Chicopee Village and had enjoyed the oversight of every mother in the community. Each child was protected, disciplined and loved by all the mothers as if they were one family. That did not, however, prevent mischief.

There was a special feel to life in The Village. For some it was simply the beauty of the surrounding landscape and views. For others it was an opportunity to participate in vibrant activities that were part of the planned community, to interact with folks who are in a similar age group, to understand the challenges and benefits of other residents and to feel part of a community.

As a young boy, Billy took full advantage of every benefit of village life. On this day he grabbed a friend and headed to the ball field. It was a perfect day for outdoor activity. Their game started in thirty minutes, but they wanted to get a head start on everyone else by hitting a few balls before the rest of the team arrived. The walk from home was less than a mile and the sidewalks were shaded by tree-lined streets, which kept the hot July sun at bay. crepe myrtles were blooming along the road with roses, petunias, and other bedding plants filling the pine straw in each planting bed. He loved the feeling of belonging that the village provided, the friends he had made, and the opportunity to stay as active as he wanted.

He could see a group of spectators already gathering at the ball field, as he passed the tennis courts. Neighbors were calling out to each other and joking about their escapades of the day. Some residents were walking their dogs. Others were stopping to talk. It was great to be a ten-year old in Chicopee Village, Gainesville, Georgia, in 1954. Life there was somewhat different than life in the fifty-five and older Village where Loraine and Billy lived now. But for Billy, the design of a planned community offered the same sense of belonging that is inherent in any village.

In 1926-27 Chicopee Mill and Village was built on Walnut Creek Watershed by Johnson & Johnson as a premier community. The Mill was located on the west side of Atlanta Hwy 13 and the Village on the east side. The mill, village and all ancillary land encompassed over 500 acres. It was the first one-story, light-filled textile mill with modern conveniences in the country. It looked like a college campus. After the manufacturing mill was completed, the company began working with local farmers from Hall, Jackson, Barrow and Gwinnett counties to experiment with cotton. The mill produced cheese cloth, gauze and other medical supplies for soldiers in WWI England. By 1953 a finishing plant was added, in 1966 a baby products plant opened, and in 1967 a plant for yarn and weaving completed the complex. Early on, the company began a project to reforest the land surrounding the mill to recover trees that had been used to build the homes in the Village. A large filtration plant was built to produce drinking water for the community. Chicopee was a self-contained environmentally aware village, where health, safety, well-being and quality of life were a primary concern of the company.

The community provided life-changing amenities in the 250 homes for mill employees with 31 different layouts for them to choose from with the first indoor plumbing, hot water and electricity with unprecedented buried wiring underground. Streets were curbed and paved, with street lights illuminating sidewalks at night. The homes were four-side brick with screens on the windows and solid wood floors. To assure that employees were provided with everything needed for daily life, there was a grocery store, barber shop, beauty shop, post office, florist, and doctor's office facing Atlanta Hwy 13 on a town-center fully landscaped green area.   Scattered throughout the community was a filling station, community center with juke box, ball field, swimming pool, tennis court, shuffleboard court, Boy Scout club house, school, and churches.

To a person, everyone who grew up in the village felt that they were part of a large family, were blessed to have the opportunities it offered and declare that it was the greatest place in the world to grow up in.   Faces light up with memories of life in this small town village of yesteryear.   Stories of mischief, achievement, caring and grief are shared at every gathering of folks from this community. Doctors, lawyers, judges and entrepreneurs were spawned by this Village. Every funeral for a former resident is attended by dozens of men and women who were part of the larger family. As is the case for most decade-old communities, houses have become worn and unkempt.   Tree roots have pushed up sidewalks.   Shrubs have grown into unmanageable foliage. And poorly designed additions have erased the simple beauty of the original craftsman-style. However, over the past few years, a new energy has emerged with new owners refurbishing the homes and bringing life back to the community.

130

Billy and his friends hoped that this redevelopment would continue and that Chicopee Village could once again become a viable community.

Today, Billy was retelling the story about the day the four of them had gathered a basket of tomatoes one of the men in the community had grown. They sat on a grassy knoll overlooking the road leading to the corner store. As a delivery truck left the store, they each picked up a tomato and threw it at the truck, plastering the windshield with sticky red juice. The truck slowed and the boys ducked behind the berm. The truck slowly drove away stopping occasionally to let the driver peer into the woods. He never saw them. This gave the boys a boost of bravado. So, the next truck was headed toward the store. The boys figured they would have more time to completely cover the windshield with tomato splatter. They each grabbed three tomatoes and as the truck slowed to make the turn into the store, they all bombarded the truck with their harmless weapons. To their amazement the truck driver stopped the truck in the middle of the street, reached under the seat and jumped out with a gun pointing in their direction. In disbelief they began running deeper into the woods, except for the runt of the group. Donnie's short legs kept him from moving as fast. When he looked back to make sure the driver wasn't following, he ran smack into a huge oak tree. The laughter that rang out from the office rivaled the laughter they shared that day as they crept forward to check on Donnie, who was completely knocked out.

131

It felt good to hear Billy laughing again. He always had a sense of humor about things that happened to him when he was a child. She wished he could keep this positive attitude when the guys left.

The visit tired Billy to the point that she knew he would sleep all afternoon. "Honey will you be okay if I go visit Mom for a little while this afternoon?"

"Yes. I'm probably going to sleep anyway."

It had always amazed Loraine that he could fall asleep so easily. Even before his surgery, he could close his eyes sitting up or lying down and be asleep in a couple of minutes and sleep through television noise or outside commotion. He rarely took a pain pill to relieve his discomfort.

35.

Kathryn was excited to go into Atlanta with Peggy and Martha the night of the competition. The contest was sponsored by a local radio station that had rented out the ballroom on the second floor of the Fox Theatre.

Traffic was gridlocked for blocks around the theater. Kathryn drank in the energy and excitement from the hustle of people walking arm-in-arm on the streets, and the lights coming from the tall buildings' windows, streetlights spotlighting cone-shaped areas on sidewalks that featured foot traffic as they walked under each light and the collision of headlights from the cars traveling in all directions. She was mesmerized by it all. She wanted to stay here forever.

But the competition started at 7:00 p.m. So there was no time to dally on the walk from the parking lot to the inside of the theater. To her amazement, the Fox was as breathtaking as the light-show outside. The thick red carpet ran from the front door to the entrance of the theater seating in long strips across the porcelain gold embellished designed floor. She had never seen anything like it. The ceiling must have been 40 or 50 feet high with chandeliers containing hundreds of small lights sending twinkles of yellow rays down on the floor.

Kathryn wanted to go into the seating area, but there was not enough time. Instead she was steered to the left and up a grandiose set of steps to the ballroom where contestants were converging on each set of massive double doors leading into the ballroom.

Seeing the number of competitors made her stomach flip over. She could have never competed alone. Martha and Peggy gave her the courage and confidence to do this. They had chosen simple cotton dresses with a small floral print on each in contrasting colors and banded short sleeves. The bodice was fitted loosely but snugly at the waist and flowed to below the knees in a triangular cut which swung easily as they moved. Hose and chunky heels along with wide-brimmed hats with one side pinned up with ribbon bands matching the floral colors in their dresses completed their attire.

The night flew by for the sisters. They were comfortable performing in front of large audiences at church. This was an entirely different situation. In all there were 25 acts competing. Unbelievably they made it to the final three. Each of the last three acts had to perform another song. The sisters had not rehearsed another number for the night, but decided they had sung "Boogie-woogie Bugle Boy" so many times they could pull it off.

They brought the house down. Immediately they each were given a $100 bill, a dozen yellow roses, gift certificates to Rich's Department Store, coupons for free meals at Davis Brothers Cafeteria on Luckie Street in downtown Atlanta, and the big prize--six months of weekly performances on the local radio station which paid them each nicely.

Kathryn's love affair with Atlanta was sealed. The six months that Martha, Peggy and Kathryn spent preparing for their weekly 15-minute shows and the trips to Atlanta to perform brought them close again. Kathryn missed the easy banter with Frank and Bill, but formed a new respect for her two sisters. Bud drove them to Atlanta each week for their show, waited on them to perform and then drove them back to Griffin. Kathryn learned to respect Bud even more and enjoyed his quiet nature and willingness to help them with transportation. But her favorite part of the drive was looking at the skyline of Atlanta. The lights, traffic and energy pulsing out of every block in the city gave her deep satisfaction.

She knew she wanted to live there, when the six months were over.

36

Winning the contest was the first positive moment in Kathryn's life in a long time. She had dropped out of high school her last year to go to business school. She knew she must have a skill in order to get a good job. It turned out that her piano lessons had taught her how to move her fingers independently which made typing a cinch for her. However, the commute back and forth to the school kept her tired and uninterested in anything social when she got home at night.

She had missed prom and graduation, which were important for teenage girls. But Kathryn had carried with her the shame of her family's disgrace when Henry was asked to leave Covington because of Peggy's pregnancy. She felt disapproving eyes on her everywhere she went even though they weren't there. People in Griffin didn't know of her family's past. She couldn't shake the feeling of unworthiness and ugliness because she had worn dresses to school that Ola painstakingly made of flour sack cloth. She knew the other girls made fun of her looks and her dresses. So she shied away from any contact that was not necessary for school.

Business school was better but she felt she had missed out on something that other girls took for granted. Winning the singing contest meant that she, Martha and Peggy would see each other at least once a week to practice and then another time to perform at the radio station. While that was exciting, spending time with her sisters was more important to her. Family always came first.

Before the six-month contract for the radio show was up, Martha was getting impatient with the commitment it took. She was working full time; practicing and doing the show each week took time away from Charles, whom she lovingly called Charlie. She was happy with the extra money she made though. It would help with expenses setting up a home with him.

During this busy time, Martha and Ola had planned her spring wedding. Henry contributed by designing a temporary aisle from the back porch into the back yard where a pagoda was built for the bride and groom to recite their vows. Each side of the aisle was lined with daylilies interspersed with petunias and in the center fresh mulch was carefully laid, packed and overlaid with white sheets for the bride's safety. Baskets of ferns, irises and roses adorned each side of the pagoda. The background was filled with dozens of **gladiolas**. Tables with white tablecloths were set up for cake and punch after the ceremony. Ola baked the 3 layer wedding cake and Peggy used her connections at the lunch counter to make a pink punch with creamy ice cream. Attendance was limited to family and long-time friends, assuring the intimacy Martha and Charles wanted. There was no honeymoon immediately. The couple planned to travel to Daytona Beach, Florida, after the commitment to the radio show was completed.

Susan and Tom attended, obviously still starry-eyed with each other. Earl and Muriel arrived arm-in-arm. Frank received a weekend pass and showed up just in time for the ceremony. The family was all together again, celebrating their love and connection to each other.

Peggy felt guilty leaving Dick with Bud so much after he had worked all day at the garage. But the extra money also made her feel like she was contributing to their household. They had moved into a garage apartment after they married at the courthouse. It had two small bedrooms and a kitchen nook behind the living room and one bath. It was small, but it was theirs and they were happy. Peggy did not resent the celebratory commotion focused on Martha and her wedding. She was happy that Martha lived her life in a way to realize the dream all the sisters had as young girls

The show stirred Kathryn's love for music again and she began writing some tunes in her head. She wasn't proficient in reading or writing music. So she couldn't put anything on paper, but she could remember each note of each song.

Music was her first love. Atlanta was her second. She came alive when she approached the tall buildings, bustling crowds and commotion of cars and trollies moving non-stop through the city. The experience was one she never tired of. She dreamed that one day she would move there and live the rest of her life among the hustle and bustle.

Griffin was a nice town but the ache in her heart was for Atlanta.

Ralph and Bill were still working at the mattress factory and had become friends with some of the guys who worked there. They formed a baseball team and played workers from other factories in the town. Bill tried to get Kathryn to attend the games just to get her out some. She wasn't really interested, but one night Bill, Ralph and the girls they were dating decided to go to the skating rink. They asked Kathryn to go along. It seemed like a nice change from her normal evenings, so she said okay.

When they arrived at the rink, they bumped into their boss's son, Roy, who was leaving. Bill encouraged him to stay and skate with them. "Roy, we've brought my sister down here and she needs a partner to skate with. Can you hang around for a while?"

Roy took one look at Kathryn and was immediately immersed in her dark brown, round, innocent eyes and decided it was worth staying a little longer so he could get to know her. Kathryn blushed and said, "You have to forgive my brother. He doesn't know how to act appropriately. Don't feel pressured to stay on my account. I've skated by myself for a long time. I can manage."

"It isn't an inconvenience at all. I need the extra exercise. I was leaving because I was bored being here alone. Besides I didn't know those characters had a sister. Now, you can tell me all about

139

them. I need some dirt on them. They are always pulling some prank on the other guys at work."

"If I told you what you want to know, they might get fired." She smiled at him.

That night was the beginning of their romance. They were together every night until Roy proposed.

37

Loraine walked through the lobby of the assisted living, smiling as she moved from the front door to the hallway leading to Kathryn's room. Some residents were sitting along the hall staring out at the garden; some were visiting with other residents and some were slumped in their wheelchairs, head down and chin on chest. She tried to make eye contact with each one and smile. Occasionally, a resident would smile back or say hello. Most of the time, they never indicated that they saw her.

Her heart ached for the lives that had been vibrant and productive and now seemed to be thrown away and empty. The consolation for them was the fact that they were being well-taken care of. They were cooked three meals a day, had two snacks, laundry done, and a healthcare professional administer medicine and take care of personal needs daily. The garden setting sheltered them from the busy main road where traffic rushed past, taking occupants to work, home and other places. There were common areas with comfortable sofas and chairs and large screen televisions, an exercise room, hobby room, chapel and dining rooms to challenge some upscale restaurants. But it was not home.

The staff referred to it as the residents' home, and it was where they lived. But it lacked one main ingredient: family. Most residents accepted their new surroundings and made the best of it. Some family visited. Some family members ate a meal or two each week with their moms or dads. Everyone had their own rooms where they had personal furniture and important accessories, family pictures and books. The important papers were kept by a relative outside of the facility and most furniture they had cherished over the years was sold at yard or estate sales.

As she walked down the hallway she hoped that a smile and a kind gesture could help make the day brighter for a resident. She wanted someone to be kind to Kathryn in that way. She observed her mom trying to be friendly with other residents, but to Loraine this was something new in Kathryn's personality. She had always thought of her mother as shy and introverted. She knew it must be difficult for her to speak first to other people. Selfishly, she had always wanted Kathryn to make friends, so that she wouldn't feel so guilty that Kathryn had to spend much of her life alone. Now that she was living in a place where she saw the same people every day she could make them a part of her social life. Would she?

Loraine thought about the years she and her siblings had arranged their lives to be with Kathryn every holiday. Some years it was difficult to get everyone together, but they always managed. Even though they did not live close to each other, the one to two-and-a-half hour drives each way were a tribute to their love for their mom. Loraine remembered the years after her divorce from her sons' dad, when she would sometimes feel so overwhelmed with the responsibility of raising the boys and making every decision about them, while working a full-time job and finishing her college degree.

She called Kathryn any time of day or night and always received understanding and love from her. There was never any judgment or unwanted advice. There was just a listening ear and loving comments that things would be okay because she believed that Loraine was smart and ambitious, but most of all, devoted to her two sons and with God's help, she could get beyond her current circumstances.

These memories made Loraine so grateful for her mother. She was determined to do whatever she needed to do to make her last years comfortable and happy.

Loraine opened the door to Kathryn's room. "Hi Mom."

Kathryn was asleep in her recliner. It was about an hour before lunch. Loraine hated to wake her up, but she didn't want to waste their time together. She leaned over and touched Kathryn's arm. Kathryn jerked and opened her eyes, a frightened look on her face.

"Oh, I'm sorry I scared you. But I thought you would want us to visit, rather than for me to watch you sleep."

"I'm so glad you did. I've missed you. How long can you stay? How is Billy?"

The hour went by fast. Kathryn entreated her to stay for lunch, but the dining rooms were so crowded that there was no space for her to sit at her mom's table and the noise would have prevented them from talking. Kathryn's hearing had gotten so bad that she had a hard time hearing in a quiet room when she sat next to you. Loraine pushed her wheelchair out to the veranda and they talked in the warm sun. Kathryn pulled her sweater closer. "I'm cold."

"Okay. I thought you might like to sit in the sun a little. It is such a beautiful fall day. But we can go inside."

Loraine settled Kathryn at her table for lunch, kissed her on the cheek and told her she would see her soon. As she drove home she thought about her mom's life and how she had struggled with the "shame" she felt, never thinking she could live her life with her values and morals attesting to who she was. Loraine began to contrast her own feelings of being outside the circle of her friends with her mother's feelings of not measuring up. Could it be that her timidity about joining in with the girlfriends was based on her feelings of inferiority?

She had always felt ill at ease with her friends. She never shared her feelings, likes or dislikes. When they were giggling over name brand clothes, shoes and purses, she was hoping to get a new outfit regardless of who made it. When they were scheming over how to attract a certain boy in their class, she wasn't interested. She felt years older than most of her classmates. When a carload of girls left from school together and planned a trip to the Varsity that night, she rushed home to stay with her grandmother until Mom got home. And four nights a week she worked at the neighborhood library to earn a little money so she could put gas in the hand-me-down car she drove to school

She never wanted to be the center of attention. Yet, she ran for Co-President of the student body in high school. Even though she won the election, she felt it was somehow by default. She tried every challenge presented to her. When she won, she had that same feeling that it was by default. When she lost, she felt that it was inevitable. She wasn't worthy.

She put on a cheerful face and laughed or kidded her way out of every disappointment. She was well-known at school for her laugh. She shared Kathryn's dry sense of humor. But she was naïve in so many ways. When a conversation was going a certain way, she would interject a thought or question that was way off-base from the other comments. She was analytical and introspective but she didn't know how to talk to other people to become part of the group. She embarrassed herself many times in groups when her response was considered inappropriate for the situation. She never realized that she was not living a genuine life. Not until now.

38

Kathryn couldn't believe that she had met someone she respected and felt so comfortable with. They talked about all their hopes and dreams and the desire to have a home and children. They were both shy and cautious but they were in love. The war was escalating in Europe, but that seemed so far away. Roy's proposal was a predictor of what life would be like for them.

There was no fanfare, no big surprise, and no large engagement ring. But there **was** an engagement ring, one that Kathryn would wear the rest of her life. It had a ¼ carat round cut diamond in a squared setting with two diamond slivers on each side. It fit her slim finger perfectly. Roy took Kathryn to dinner at the local diner, and when they arrived back at her house, he pulled out the ring and asked her if she would be his for the rest of their lives. There was no hesitation. She threw her arms around his neck and said yes. They met in December 1939 and married in June 1940.

Kathryn's life was happy when she met and married Roy after only six months of dating. During the six-month engagement, Kathryn had come to love the rest of Roy's family. They were gracious, kind, accepting of her and were delighted that Roy had found the love of his life. Roy's sisters were eager to tell Kathryn all about their big brother. They were so proud of him. He had been a straight "A" student all through school, but in the eleventh grade he became sick and couldn't seem to shake the infection. He was treated for a lung disease and went to the Alto Sanatorium in the north Georgia Mountains for six months to recover. However, when he returned home he was very weak and was unable to finish high school. His dad ordered a correspondence course in electronics for him. As usual, he absorbed all the information and built a short wave radio where he listened to messages from ships.

That setback didn't thwart his curiosity and desire to continuously "engineer" projects. When they were 14 and 12, Roy and his younger brother, Horace, pulled together car pieces and built one for themselves. They drove it all over Griffin and would let Elizabeth (their younger sister) ride in a wooden crate substituting for a back seat. He designed and built a television set, long before one came on the market. Anything electronic intrigued him. But his desire to figure out how things worked wasn't limited to electronics. As teenagers, he and Horace took old wheels off street skates the other kids discarded and built riding toys, boxcars, skateboards and small pedal cars.

The Noble Giles Mauney family moved from Mitchell County, North Carolina to Greensboro, Georgia. Arthur and Algie Lee were next door neighbors in Greensboro. Roy's dad, Arthur LeRoy Mauney, attended business school, where he learned typing and shorthand. He worked in the Clerk's Office in the Courthouse in Greensboro. He married Algie

Lee Perkins in 1912. Beulah, their first child, was born in Greensboro, Georgia, in 1914. Roy was born in Greensboro in 1916.

The Arthur Mauney family moved many times during the first years of their marriage trying to find jobs during the depression. Eventually, Arthur's dad, Noble Giles Mauney used his engineering degree knowledge earned at Rutherford College, North Carolina, to start a mattress factory in Greensboro with his brother, Horace (later called Big Horace after Roy's brother Horace was born). There was a great need for replacement mattresses for hospitals, hotels and the armed forces. And with no opportunities to continue his job as a machinist at the mill, this seemed like a good option.

The mattress factory had its ups and downs, moving the family from Greensboro to West Palm Beach, Florida, back to Greensboro, Georgia, and eventually Arthur moved the family to Griffin, Georgia, where he started his own mattress factory. Roy and Horace worked with their dad in the business.

His family was similar in size to Kathryn's. There were five sons and three daughters. Roy and his older sister Beulah had set to work after high school to earn enough money to pay for the younger siblings' college. They sacrificed a future professional life that each of them could have had. The four other brothers, Horace, John, Art and Dick graduated from Georgia Tech in Atlanta. Elizabeth attended a local college and Barbara (Bobbie) attended Shorter College in Rome, Georgia on a voice scholarship. There she met her future husband, Bill Gaines.

The Mauney family was well-respected in Griffin and was a big part of The First Baptist Church. Beulah played the piano/organ for the church and Bobbie sang many solos over the years.

Kathryn learned about the mattress business from Roy as they sat in their bedroom in the Mauney house each night. She also learned that the Mauneys had moved around as much as her family in order to earn a living. This knowledge somehow eased her fears about being rejected by his family, since they had been as unsettled as her family. The haunting shame about Peggy's pregnancy outside of marriage was eased by the shame Roy felt about not finishing high school and attending college. In those days tuberculosis was seen as an outcast disease because of its infectious nature. Roy was ashamed as well as disappointed about not attending college. He loved learning and was a cerebral man who enjoyed finding solutions to problems. His quiet nature and dry sense of humor matched Kathryn's perfectly.

She looked up to him and adored him the rest of her life. They had an intimate ceremony at the Justice of the Peace and celebrated with both families afterward at the Mauney residence in Griffin.

They moved in with her in-laws because they had to save up for a deposit on an apartment. Algie Lee was a straight-laced woman who ran her house like a business but had a warm, loving heart. She accepted life as it was presented to her and learned how to adapt to whatever circumstance she must face. She supported Arthur all the years he ran the mattress factory by sewing the mattress covers. Her sister-in-law, Bessie, worked beside her and they managed household and business matters with no complaints. The whole country was adjusting to living with less and working harder. They were thankful that they had a means of supporting their families.

Living under her mother-in-law's roof had its challenges for Kathryn, especially the following year (1941) when Janice Kathryn Mauney was born. She was a beautiful baby but colic kept her and Kathryn awake almost every night and Kathryn feared the rest of the family too. She yearned for a place of their own, regardless of how small.

Kathryn looked out the window of their bedroom into the back yard. She was so thankful that Mr. and Mrs. Mauney had welcomed her and Roy into their home. The house sat behind two large Mimosa trees in the center of the 2 acre lot, which was level from front to rear. Water birch trees bowed down to the strawberry patch in the rear of the lot. The green lawn was kept neat and trim by a teenage boy in the neighborhood. Kathryn felt guilty for wanting to leave this peaceful setting, but she needed to have her own space. When Roy returned from work, she met him at the door with Janice in her arms.

"Can we talk?"

"Sure. Are you okay?"

As he closed the door to their room, she put Janice in the crib and looked up at him with teary eyes. "Not really. I'm feeling so out of place here. Your parents have been wonderful to us, but I'm always afraid that we're making too much noise and at night Janice cries and keeps everyone awake. I'm on edge all day and all night."

Roy put his arms around her and drew her close. "I know honey. I feel the same way. We need to find a place just for us. I've been saving some money from my paycheck each week to put a down payment on an apartment. I almost have enough, but we need to find an inexpensive place. I wanted to surprise you with this decision, but I know you need to make a change now. We'll start looking this weekend. You can check the paper each day for available places."

Once again Roy had already recognized the problem and found a solution. She was such a blessed woman.

39.

Arthur's mattress company had ups and downs just as his dad's had. In the midst of a downturn Arthur decided he needed to close the factory. The war had helped at first because of the need for bedding for drafted servicemen and women. The ranks of the services grew swiftly and constantly for months and years until the military draft finally caught up with Roy.

He was sent to basic training at Warner Robins, Georgia, and served there for almost a year. Kathryn and Janice went with him. They rented a small apartment on the base and began their core family life. Kathryn was happy. She loved setting up her own kitchen, bedrooms and living room with hand-me-down furniture. The only thing important was to be with Roy and keep the family together. Algie Lee and Arthur visited when they could. They were both getting older and found it hard to make the trip from Griffin to Warner Robins.

Beulah had moved to Thomaston, Georgia, years earlier, after her husband was killed in a car accident. She worked as a court reporter and made a good living for herself. As things got harder for Algie Lee and Arthur she sent them money to supplement their needs. She took over the mortgage on the house they had built so that they could have stability in their lives.

It was not uncommon for entire families to work in business together. When Arthur and Algie Lee married, she and Arthur's sister, Bess, took over the job of sewing mattress covers. They worked wherever they could find a place, keeping pace with the men's production of mattress frames and pads. As the business moved from place to place, at one point they worked out of a barn on Big Horace's land. Algie Lee walked home after a hard day's work, which began at 5 a.m., and cooked dinner for her large family. There was never time nor money for vacations or long breaks of any kind. They had to produce while the work was there.

During the profitable times, after they moved the business to Griffin, Arthur and Algie Lee built a white clapboard home on a level lot of approximately two acres. There were two mature Mimosa trees in the front yard shading the front of the house and a prolific strawberry garden in the back yard. This was a favorite place for the grandchildren to hang out. They had sufficient money to furnish the home with Duncan Phyfe furniture, a piano, and comfortable furniture in the den and on the screened-in porch. Over the years, family get-togethers filled the home, porch and yards with laughter and sibling and cousin teasing. These were the good years.

40

Barbara Loraine Mauney was born in Warner Robins on the military base on January 27, 1944. Shortly thereafter, Roy was reassigned to Japan. Kathryn had no ties to Warner Robins. So, when Roy left for Japan, she finally got her opportunity to move to Atlanta. She needed a job to supplement Roy's service pay. Housing was sparse during the war years. It took months for Kathryn to find a house for her and the girls. Fortunately, Peggy and Bud also wanted to move to Atlanta where mechanic jobs were easier to find. They moved in with Kathryn in the small two bedroom, six room home in the close community of East Atlanta. As payment for their share of the mortgage payments, Peggy took care of the girls while Kathryn worked as a switchboard operator at Western Union.

Each morning, Kathryn walked the eight blocks to the bus line for the ride into Atlanta and retraced her steps each evening. It was a hard time for the family, because the dream of a home with Roy in Atlanta had been replaced with a home that now housed Peggy, Bud, Dick, Ralph and Bill. Ralph and Bill moved to Atlanta to find better jobs, but couldn't find a place to rent or buy. Peggy and Bud had one bedroom. Kathryn, Janice and Loraine had the other bedroom. Ralph, Bill and Dick slept in the dining room and living room. The days were long for Kathryn, but her good nature and work ethic kept her going. Besides, she got an adrenalin rush as she traveled on the bus and streetcars to downtown Atlanta each day

She loved the activity of folks rushing to work in the early morning, stopping for a cup of coffee and donut at the Krystal on cold, rainy mornings. In those days, people smiled at each other as they passed on the streets. They helped each other with packages and slippery sidewalks in the winter ice. They held doors open for each other. They were happy that they were alive and working.

As the war began to wind down, more housing was built around the country. Levitt and Sons, a large construction company in Pennsylvania, built the first pre-fab subdivision and called it Levitt Town to accommodate the servicemen and women returning from war and looking for a place to live. Housing starts grew in the Atlanta area too and relieved the crowded living arrangements of residents in the surrounding areas. This resulted in the family living next door to Kathryn moving to a new home in a nearby subdivision. Ralph and Bill decided to buy the home and moved Ola and Henry in with them. Henry was suffering from emphysema and only had enough energy to move from bed to sofa to rocking chair on the front porch. When he passed away, Ola continued living with her sons until Ralph married and brought his wife into the home.

The arrangement was not the best for either of the brothers. It was the perfect opportunity for Bill to bow out, take what personal items fit on his Harley-Davidson motorcycle and head to Daytona Beach, his dream destination. He had been traveling to Daytona several times a year for a long time, making sure he was there for the Daytona Beach 500 automobile race.

Kathryn was sensitive to the appearance this living situation gave to the neighbors. Other families in the neighborhood were typical husband, wife and children in the home. There was not the activity surrounding those homes that the Mauney house necessitated. Embarrassed feelings began to surface once again for Kathryn. She felt that she didn't belong in this community of bankers, lawyers, policemen, business owners and stay-at-home moms. She had nothing in common with them and so she didn't make the effort to get to know any of the other women.

Work was a different matter. She worked with other women who gave her the interaction she needed outside the home. They accepted their role of provider for their families while their husbands served the country and had fun working, teasing each other, and earning much-needed income. Besides, the job allowed Kathryn to travel each day to her beloved Atlanta.

She came alive on the walk to the bus stop. She didn't mind the cold mornings, the bus fumes, the noise and congestion on the bus or the occasional times that she had to stand on the 12-mile ride. When she exited the bus many mornings, her first stop was the Krystal restaurant where the windows were fogged over from the warmth inside, and the talking and laughter floated out to the street as she opened the door. Saving pennies meant that, rather than eating a full breakfast, she would order a cup of coffee and two doughnuts to go.

Her love for music was a constant in her life. As she became comfortable with her co-workers, she developed a close relationship with another young woman who also had grown up in a musical family. They used breaks and lunch time to share their dreams about music. Over time, this sharing developed into a plan to write songs together. Kathryn had no trouble composing the music to their first endeavor, but she did not have the skill to put her tune to sheet music. Sandra wrote the words to fit the music perfectly and was eager to get it to a producer. She suggested that Kathryn sing the song on a tape recorder because Sandra had a friend who could translate the music to musical notes on sheet music. Kathryn was happy Sandra had this solution which could make the song marketable.

Months went by and Sandra began making excuses to Kathryn about the delay in getting her a copy of the sheet music. Being trusting and naïve Kathryn didn't push the issue. Eventually, Sandra quit her job and disappeared. Kathryn never heard from her again and assumed that Sandra had taken the song as her own and promoted it to a producer. Missing an opportunity to create a song that could be heard by the public was a disappointment that Kathryn never got over. But her disappointment in Sandra confirmed her belief that trusting other people outside her family was a mistake.

41

Roy couldn't wait to get home to Kathryn and the girls. When he finally made it to 1385 Ormwood Avenue, he was disappointed with the curb-appeal, or lack thereof, of his new home. There was a sturdy sidewalk throughout the neighborhood, but the front yard of the house gradually sloped away from the sidewalk to the backyard which ended in a creek in some deep woods. To the left of the house the driveway also sloped down and ended in a detached garage. This feature had been an advantage when Kathryn bought the house, because it offered storage for furniture she and Peggy and Bud could not fit into the house.

When Roy returned from Japan, the house was much too crowded with Peggy, Bud and Dick there. He wasn't happy with the house, its white asbestos shingles, sloped yard and busy street. But he understood that Kathryn didn't have a choice of where to live when she moved to Atlanta. No one would rent to a woman with children. So, she purchased the home for $5,000 and paid a mortgage payment of $50 a month.

Upon opening the door, Roy was greeted with wall to wall furniture and people, not all his immediate family. The excitement of seeing the girls and Kathryn again immediately removed any disappointment he had felt when he first arrived. Wonderful aroma flowed to the front door from the kitchen. A feast had been prepared for his homecoming. The dining room barely held all nine residents. It was apparent that having him at home was going to change living arrangements for Ralph, Bill, Peggy, Bud and Dick.

The celebration lasted only one night. Kathryn had to get up early the next morning and set out for Atlanta and her job at Western Union. The discharge pay Roy received would not carry them for long without her salary. At first Roy looked for work near home. But there were so many veterans coming home at the same time that jobs were scarce. The economy was improving, but jobs were slow to develop.

Within a month of Roy's return the family next door decided to buy a new house and put their home up for sale. Ralph and Bill saw this as the perfect opportunity to invest in real estate and move Ola and Henry from Griffin to Atlanta where there would be family to look after them. Bud and Peggy found a garage apartment a few blocks away and moved there so they could finally have a home for themselves and Dick. Over the years, Bud was able to save enough money to build a small four-side brick home for Peggy. She was overwhelmed at his devotion to her and always struggled with her guilt of the position she had put her family in when she became pregnant. She carried her feeling of unworthiness with her to her grave.

Roy stayed in touch with three friends he had made in the Army Air Corps. They were having the same issues finding jobs. One day when they met for coffee, they discussed building a business together. They were all electronic/electrical experts. So, the company would have to use those skills.

Even though people were struggling to make ends meet and cut back on food to accommodate their reduced budget, everyone was so hopeful since the war ended that music permeated every aspect of their lives. It was the mid 40's and music was an important part of daily life from jazz to swing, from the big bands and finally to soul and then jitterbug. The four men agreed on the idea to bring music to every diner and restaurant within a manageable area around East Atlanta by renting and placing juke boxes in these gathering places. The name, "**Sam, Roy, Mack and Jack**", fit the country's attitude and their lighthearted approach to business.

The juke box company was a fun and exciting change for Roy. Instead of being tied to one location all day, he and his partners were out with customers, either delivering the equipment, updating the records within the box, replacing worn or cracked records or picking up boxes when customers no longer wanted them. The rest of their days were spent servicing the boxes and doing paperwork to run the financial part of the business.

Roy was relaxed and easygoing and this type of life allowed him to unwind from the stress of the war. World War II had changed the country for the good. People appreciated the little that they had and enjoyed just being with family and attending church. It was a grateful country. Even though jobs were not all that plentiful, men accepted whatever work they could find. At least it was easier than the Depression had been.

Two years after Roy's return, Kathryn gave birth to a son, Donald Eugene Mauney and she was able to stay home with him, Janice and Loraine. She was relieved of the responsibility of making all the decisions for the family and gladly gave up all control to Roy. He made the money and kept to the budget. Kathryn never wanted to be the decision-maker and was happy the rest of their marriage letting Roy take charge. He included her in all major decisions, but she looked up to him, believed he was the "head of the home" and deferred to his decisions as was the norm for most couples during this time. The two bedroom house was getting crowded with five members, but they made the decision that Kathryn would not return to work at Western Union after Don's birth. Kathryn asked Roy for them to start looking for a larger home, but he was hesitant to get into debt. Eventually, they decided to enclose the screened-in porch for Don's room since the girls could share a bedroom.

Life was good for the family. Bill, Ralph and Ola lived next door, Henry died in 1950 from emphysema; Peggy and Bud lived nearby; so, there was a constant flow of family visiting their home. Roy and Sam and their families spent time together as much as possible outside of work. Eventually the juke box became only a novelty. Restaurants began to struggle and had to cancel rentals of the juke box. More families were buying record players and records were available at reasonable prices. It was a smarter decision to buy a record that could be played as often as wanted, rather than spend money on a song that was heard only once. Dance clubs were opening where customers could hear music and dance while they ate and drank.

Many military servicemen and women were accustomed to the entertainment provided by the USO while they were on active duty and looked forward to nights spent at dance clubs.

The company was successful for a few years, but as more families were able to afford record players for home use, eating out became more about visiting and conversing than reveling in the music. It just couldn't support four families. Roy was looking for a sound job with health and retirement benefits, and Sam had been having health issues. So Roy and Sam sold their interest in the business to Mack and Jack. The decision to sell his share in the business was hard for Roy. Giving up something he loved for the unknown was a hard adjustment for his temperament. But when Sam was diagnosed with a bleeding ulcer and quickly passed away, Roy knew that was a sign from God for him to look for a job that provided health insurance and retirement. Sam's hospital bills were astronomical and his wife and children were struggling. The business tried to pick up some of the cost, but there was little there to recover. After Sam's death, it was hard for Roy to stay in touch with his wife.

42

Calling on his natural skills and knowledge learned in the Army Air Corps, Roy returned to working on airplanes in Conley, Georgia, and then at Lockheed in northwest Atlanta. He and Kathryn lived in the house until all the children were married. Roy interviewed with an airplane company that built military planes at Conley, Georgia, and accepted a "swing-shift" job that provided the basics of what he was looking for, except that he was working while the family slept and sleeping while Kathryn worked and the girls were in school.

Life became routine until Ralph married and Bill decided to move to Florida. That required a new decision about where Ola would live. Henry had died from emphysema several years earlier and Ola had broken her hip and had limited mobility, using a walker and eventually a wheelchair. Ola moved in with Kathryn and Roy. This move necessitated another bedroom. There was a long narrow porch on the back of the house that was converted to a bedroom for Janice and a breakfast room. Loraine shared her bedroom with her grandmother, Ola. Roy always asserted that he hated the house, but they added two more bedrooms and raised their children there. He had his first heart attack in his 50's and had to take a disability retirement from Lockheed at age 58 when he experienced his second heart attack.

Building military airplanes became less necessary a few years after the end of WWII. The company at Conley lost several contracts and laid off employees, eventually closing its doors. Roy had many months of joblessness.

It became necessary for Kathryn to go back to work. Roy and Kathryn discussed the situation and without any hesitation Kathryn volunteered to go back to work. They would pay Peggy to stay with the children. She and Bud needed the money and she had no skills that would pay her enough to have someone stay with Dick. He was in school for most of the day. So it was decided that Peggy could have him ride the bus to Roy and Kathryn's house after school. Bud would pick her and Dick up when he got off work. Peggy did not drive.

Kathryn had little trouble landing a job at a large insurance company as a dictaphone operator. Her salary kept the family afloat until Roy was hired at Lockheed in Marietta, Georgia, as an Electronic Specialist and Trainer. However, his months of unemployment left him hesitant to make any large financial commitments. Even though it was evident the family needed a larger house, he couldn't make the decision to put a large debt on the family with a new mortgage. It proved to be a prudent decision, because during his twenty-year employment with Lockheed he was laid off two times for several years when the company lost government contracts. Even though he was rehired as soon as another contract was signed, he felt vulnerable to losing income for months at a time.

Life, once again, was changing for Kathryn. She accepted this burden gracefully with her good nature. As it turned out, going to work with a large insurance company in downtown Atlanta was a blessing for the family. Kathryn's experience at Western Union, her typing skills learned at business school and her good references made it easy for Hartford Insurance Company to offer her a position as a dictaphone operator. She worked in a large room with 20 or so women, reporting to various insurance executives. During these years, she made several friends who were accepting of her and became close confidants during the 18 years she worked there.

They took breaks and lunch together. They shared similar families and joked about husbands, kids, parents and life in general. It was a fun atmosphere even though they were hard-working and functioned under stressful deadlines. One of her friends, Doris, had a daughter that attended the same high school as Loraine. The other close friend, Irene, moved next door to Kathryn and Roy when they bought their brick home near I-20 in DeKalb County.

In 1965 after the three children moved out on their own, Roy and Kathryn moved into the home that they chose together. It was a four-sided brick home with a brick patio in a level yard, without central air conditioning in a stable subdivision off of I-20. He wouldn't say it, but he loved his new home. Since Kathryn was still working, he kept the yard pristine, did the grocery shopping, cleaned the house and cooked dinner every night. These were things he had never done before.

43.

And so it goes. The once tight-knit family was growing apart. Each child of Ola and Henry had dreams they needed to fulfill. Life was no longer centered on Mom and Dad. These changes were difficult for Kathryn to accept, but each person must pursue what his heart drove him to do.

For Ralph and Bill it was completing their draft responsibilities in the war. When Ralph returned home he bought a home with Bill and moved Ola and Henry in with them for a few years. Later he married and moved his wife in with them. In time, the house seemed crowded with all five members living there. It was not an ideal situation for the newlyweds. After Henry died, Bill and Ralph sold the house.

Ralph and Cathy had four children, three girls (Bonnie, Joy and Terry) and one boy (Brad). Cathy and Ralph divorced and the children lived with her. Ralph developed emphysema after his divorce and all contact with him was lost until Brad called to tell Kathryn that Ralph had died.

Bill was becoming restless too. He bought a Harley-Davidson motorcycle and left for his dream destination of Daytona Beach, Florida. He married, worked for the U.S. Post Office delivering mail and had two daughters. The family became so estranged during the ensuing years that Bill's wife never called to let Kathryn know when he passed away. When

Kathryn found out years later, she realized how fragmented the family had become. She no longer had the connection to her siblings that they shared growing up. Feelings of inadequacy for not being able to hold the family together haunted her for years.

Earl finished his education and became an insurance executive, married and had one daughter, Jenny. His wife Muriel, who was a Christian Scientist, died of breast cancer but the rest of the family didn't know it for years. Earl had a "falling out" with Kathryn over caring for Ola after Henry died. He never forgot or forgave their differences and shunned all contact with the rest of the family. When he died, his daughter notified Brad who had kept in touch with her, but Brad did not tell the rest of the family for years.

For Martha, Charlie remained the love of her life and they moved to Florida where he opened a successful jewelry business, focusing on jewelry repairs. They had three children, two girls and one boy (Dottie, Nancy and Wayne who had muscular dystrophy). Martha doted on Wayne and until his death at age 34, lifted him from bed to his wheelchair and from wheelchair to toilet and bath every day and night. Kathryn was notified by Dottie when Martha died, but she was unable to travel to attend the funeral. Charlie had died years earlier. Kathryn's family was not notified.

Peggy and Bud lived in the outskirts of Atlanta, raised Dick as a fine man who loved Bud as his own dad. He joined the air force at age 18 and when he was transferred to Texas, met the love of his life, Carolyn. When he was discharged from the Airforce, he became one of the first hires of a new company on the cutting edge of the computer revolution, Texas Instruments. He and Carolyn married and had several children. He never moved back to Georgia, but visited some. When Peggy died at an early age from emphysema, he remained in touch with Bud until he died. Dick frequently called Kathryn to check on her. He visited a couple of times before she died. On one visit, he showed Kathryn and Loraine pictures of his children and grandchildren. He was a happy man and would not change his life. He felt blessed.

His trips to Georgia were mainly to try and locate his biological father. Eventually, he found him and visited with him. He found out that Ted had remained married to Rosalie. Ted's explanation to Dick was that even though he was forced into marrying her and that she had not been pregnant, he had made a vow before God and he was bound to honor that vow. They had no children. Rosalie died after years of suffering from a crippling disease that twisted her body into extremely painful positions. Dick did not return to Georgia after that visit. When Loraine called him to tell him of Kathryn's passing, Carolyn was caught off guard and told Loraine that Dick had passed away the year before. She said that she thought the family had been notified.

Frank never left the army. He was stationed in Japan and Germany and realized that he loved to travel. He was the only family member to continue with music. He played the piano at the USO whenever he got the chance and always had a piano in his home.

When he returned to the states on leave, he always stayed with Kathryn and Roy. Those days were filled with music and laughter. He had grown to love jazz and could be heard sounding out strange combinations of notes to the beat and rhythm of his favorite jazz songs. But when Loraine's girlfriends came over, he would get them to play their favorite rock and roll music and he would dance with them to help them get comfortable with dancing before they attended the formal dances at school. For fifteen year old girls this was a special treat. He loved sharing his music with anyone who was interested.

He was stationed at Fort McPherson for a few years and moved Ola in with him during this time. When he was reassigned to Oklahoma, Ola moved in with Kathryn and Roy and their three children, where she lived until she passed away in 1964. Henry died in 1950 while he and Ola still lived with Bill and Ralph.

Frank retired from the Army while he was stationed in Oklahoma. He met a woman whose husband had passed away several years earlier. They married and he never returned to Georgia. Kathryn and Roy flew on an airplane for the first time to be at his wedding and visit with him and Von. Kathryn's relationship with Frank had always been strong and he included her in his life as much as possible, considering how many years he lived out of the country.

But Kathryn finally realized that the family she had known as a child had evolved with life's choice, when each sibling married and created their own family, as they should.

44

A doctor visit isn't usually something you look forward to, but Billy was anxious to get out of the house and hoping his catheter would be taken out today. Dr. Jones was prompt as usual and was pleased at Billy's progress. He had the nurse do a PSA test and take the catheter out.

In his usual upbeat nature Billy told the nurse, "I'm going to hug your neck. I hope I never have to have this thing again." She smiled and said that she couldn't believe that he didn't moan or grimace when she removed it.

"That discomfort was nothing compared to dragging this pouch around with me all day," he said.

When the doctor returned he said to make an appointment in a month, but call if Billy had any issues that needed his attention.

In the car, Billy was smiling and wanting to go out to eat, but was tired from the ordeal of dressing and traveling to the doctor's office. Loraine happily drove home so that he could rest and get some energy back. The following weeks were uneventful. Billy's recovery was uncomplicated, if lengthy.

Loraine was able to visit her Mom more often because she was not uneasy about Billy leaving Billy alone.

Kathryn was glad to see her each visit but always asked, "How is Billy doing? I would love to see him for myself. You know I love him like a son."

She occasionally made comments about wishing she could go home, but she didn't press the issue. Loraine always felt guilty when she said these things, but she spent her time looking after Billy and Janice had her hands full looking after Dan, whose cancer had gotten worse. The family knew it would not be long before he would pass away. The decision was made to keep that from Kathryn, fearing that the knowledge of Dan's death would cause her depression and worry that she could do nothing about.

Thanksgiving was spent at Loraine and Billy's with Kevin and Stephen. Kathryn was excited to have a day away from the assisted living home.

"It feels so good to see something besides those four walls," she said as Loraine loaded her into the car.

"Mom, you have more than four walls. You even have a beautiful veranda to spend time on. And you can go to the gathering room to watch TV if you want."

"I know, but it's not the same as it is at your house."

The first thing Kathryn said as she walked into the kitchen, "Home at last."

Loraine hugged her and said, "You know this is your home too. I wish you could live here with us, Mom."

Memories tugged at her heart. Loraine remembered the years that Ola had lived with them when she was a teenager. She shared her room with Ola, and many times resented having to accommodate Ola's wishes instead of her own. Afternoons when she came home from school, Ola would be in the room with the radio on the Atlanta Crackers baseball games. Loraine wanted to listen to the music stations playing the latest rock 'n roll music of the late 1950's. Now she remembered feeling guilty when she would resent her lack of privacy. She loved Ola and enjoyed many afternoons when she would lie on her bed after school and Ola would rub her feet for her. On these days Loraine was happy to share her day with her grandmother. Ola always listened and occasionally asked questions and laughed at the funny things Loraine described about her day.

Ola never wanted to go into a nursing home. Kathryn vowed that she would never do that to her mom. She did everything she could to keep Ola with the family. But the last month of Ola's life she became incontinent. Kathryn was working, the kids were in school and Roy went to work 30 minutes before they got home. Kathryn hired sitters to stay four hours a day to cover the times when the family was coming and going. Kathryn and the girls took care of Ola's needs in the morning before they left, while Roy was asleep. Unfortunately sitters were undependable. It

176

became impossible to take care of her. A stroke left Ola unconscious and the hospital told Kathryn that Ola had to go to a nursing home because she would be too heavy to lift and change her diapers at home. Loraine remembered how hard this decision had been on Kathryn when she had to put Ola in a nursing home. And she knew that Kathryn would never want to go to a nursing home either.

It felt different not having Jeff and Janis and the boys with them for the holidays, but they had a good visit with Kevin and Stephen. When shadows began falling in the living room, Kathryn looked at Loraine and said, "I'm ready to go back to the assisted living facility. If I don't get there soon I will miss dinner."

Loraine turned her head so Kathryn would not see her smile. She couldn't imagine where Kathryn could put any more food after the feast she had consumed just a few hours ago. But she put on her coat, helped Kathryn with her jacket and walked slowly in front of her to keep her from tripping with her walker. The closer they got to Kathryn's new home, the sadder she felt. She didn't want to return Kathryn to "that" place. But she physically could not care for her any longer. On the drive home, Loraine remembered that Kathryn had said that she wanted to go back to the "assisted living facility". She did not call it her apartment. Loraine realized that she had not fooled Kathryn into believing that she had her own apartment, but was actually in a care-taking facility. Her heart ached at the pain she felt for herself and Kathryn.

Loraine and Billy picked Kathryn up to spend Christmas with Jeff, Janis and the boys. Kathryn enjoyed watching the three boys play with the gifts Santa had brought them. They were always kind and loving to Kathryn and she adored then. But on this day, she seemed distracted and fidgety. Once again, Kathryn was anxious to get back to the assisted living facility. The day was cut short and Loraine felt a sadness about how life would never be the same for their extended family. Loraine knew that Kathryn ate well each day because she had always had a good appetite. Food was one of her pleasures in life. She looked forward to every meal and especially the ice cream in her Ensure each afternoon when she lived with Loraine and Billy.

Loraine had always envied her mom for keeping her weight down close to her weight when she was younger. It seemed she never had to count calories or exercise excessively to be slim. But today as she and Billy left Kathryn at her new home, Loraine reminisced about those early years when she first entered Georgia State College (now Georgia State University) for night classes and worked a full-time job at Southern Bell during the day. Because she was still living at home, she and Kathryn walked to the bus stop together every morning and Kathryn walked home from there every evening, as she had for most of her working life. It must have been at least a mile and a half one way. Could this be the reason Kathryn kept her weight down? Loraine wondered that maybe her self-loathing all of her life for not being able to control her weight might have been a cruel judgment she placed on herself, when it actually could have been just a result of the day to day activities and food choices she made, rather than her not being worthy.

Christmas had always been celebrated with Kathryn. Even after Roy passed away, no matter where she lived, her three children and their children arranged the day to be with her. When she had her own place, they all met there, bringing in food and rejoicing in their time together. When she could no longer keep house and rotated living with each of her children's family, everyone met at that house for their annual get together. Traditions changed when grandchildren married and had their own families and in-laws' families to accommodate. But Kathryn was never alone on Thanksgiving or Christmas. When the boys were young, Loraine occasionally wished that she could keep them home on Christmas day to enjoy their toys without rushing through the morning, packing up the car and driving an hour or more to celebrate with siblings and, most importantly, with Kathryn.

Early in 2012 Dan's cancer had taken over his body and he was confined to a hospital bed that Janice had put in the great room of their house, so he could see outside and visitors could come in the door and be with him. Kevin, Jeff and Janis went to Cartersville with Billy and Loraine to visit with him and Janice. He passed away on March 4th the day of Billy's brother-in-law's funeral. Billy's sister, Jeanette, had taken care of her husband, Charles, for several years. He had been a severe diabetic and had gotten worse year after year. Unexpectedly, he developed some tumors that worked against his diabetes. There was nothing the doctors could do for him.

Kathryn was falling frequently in the bathroom of her room at the assisted living facility. She never broke any bones, but the facility had to send her to the hospital to be checked out each time. On one lengthy visit in the ER in Gwinnett County, a month after Dan passed away, the ER doctor told Loraine that the family needed to decide what they were going to do, because Kathryn would continue to fall, be sent to the emergency room and back to the assisted living only to fall again. This situation was not good for her or the family. Loraine decided that she would have Kathryn sent to rehab in Gainesville, where she knew healthcare workers. After rehab she could be given a room in the nursing home there if need be. It took some maneuvering, but a space was found for Kathryn in Gainesville. Amazingly, she was very happy with this situation. She told Loraine that the room was beautiful and everyone was so caring and sweet.

It was typical for Kathryn to graciously adjust to any situation. She had done it all her life. She told Loraine that she knew God was looking after her and she was safe. Loraine realized how unhappy Kathryn must have been at the assisted living facility for her to think that a room with a hospital bed and television was beautiful compared to her space at the assisted living facility, where she had new bedroom furniture, chairs, family pictures on the walls, new curtains and a window overlooking a beautiful garden. There were also exercise classes for seniors every day, movies, visits from church groups regularly, a comfortable dining room and a beautician who had a shop in the facility. Loraine's guilt about putting Kathryn in an assisted living was reminiscent of Kathryn's guilt about putting Ola in a nursing home. It was like a cloud hanging over her head all the time. There had been no promises to Kathryn, but unconsciously Loraine had never intended for Kathryn to live away from her family.

As she talked with the nurse at the assisted living facility, Loraine realized that they were not going to allow Kathryn to return to the facility when she completed rehab. Loraine was concerned about where Kathryn could go after rehab discharged her.

She never had to face that dilemma, because Kathryn contracted a highly contagious infection during her third week in rehab. The nurses, aides and Loraine had to wear protective garments when they entered the room.

Kathryn was happy to see Loraine each day when she visited, but they couldn't touch or hug. It was hard to see her under those conditions. Rarely one to complain, she accepted her situation with a good nature. Kathryn started eating less and less and finally refused to eat. One morning when Loraine came to visit, Emergency Medical Tech's were parked at the entrance. When she got inside the front door, near her Mom's room she could see them rolling a stretcher into the room. She rushed forward and one of the nurses told her that Kathryn had participated in rehab earlier, but when she came back to check on her after breakfast, she was unresponsive. The EMT's could not arouse her; since she had a "Do Not Resuscitate Order" signed they could not perform CPR. They placed her on a stretcher and took her to the hospital. Loraine called Billy and followed the ambulance to the hospital.

45

While waiting for results from tests the hospital ran on Kathryn, memories of the life Kathryn had lived flooded Loraine's mind. She knew the situation didn't look good for her mom's recovery. Over the years, Loraine had asked Kathryn about her life growing up, wanting to share memories with her. Kathryn would become very harsh, "I don't want to talk about my childhood. It was a hard time for me and I don't think it does any good to relive it." The subject was closed for that day. Loraine didn't want to badger her mom, but she had a yearning to know her family's history. Inevitably she would broach the subject again with the same outcome.

Loraine couldn't help but feel frustrated at the thought that her Mom's whole life had been lived under the cloud of shame that was not hers. If Peggy's pregnancy had happened in a time when Loraine was a teenager, she would have been sent away to have the baby, the baby would have been adopted and she would have returned home to some whispering and judgment, but no condemnation. If the pregnancy had happened today, there would have been no stigma at all. She would have even been offered an abortion to take care of her "problem". Loraine knew that Peggy would have made the decision to keep the baby regardless of her circumstances. But she wished she had not suffered the rigidity of judgment from a society that placed blame and shame so easily on others. How would her Mom's life been different?

It was true that Kathryn had lived a long, healthy life surrounded by her family who loved her. All her children and grandchildren loved being around her and wanted to share in her life, even though their lives didn't allow much time for visiting her.

Roy's death had been a total shock to everyone even though he had two heart attacks in his 50's. He had not had any further problems, until one Sunday morning he took longer than usual in the bathroom. When Kathryn went to check on him, he was near death, slumped over on the toilet.

Thankfully, Kathryn's next door neighbor was a good friend from work. She ran to her house and Irene and her husband took over the situation, calling the ambulance and helping Kathryn get to the hospital. The children rushed to the hospital, but Roy had passed before they arrived. The loss was more than they could imagine. Loraine had adored Roy. She looked up to him and wanted to please him in all of her decisions. She looked for him to be proud of her. It was a time of confusion and pain. Only three months after her separation from her children's father, Loraine felt so lonely. She had no strong shoulder to lean on or to go to for comfort. She and Kathryn became closer as they both mourned for Roy and felt loneliness beyond belief.

For a few months, Kathryn was lost without Roy. He had done everything for her in the past few years. She was confused about where important papers were, how to plan his funeral or what she would do after the funeral. Fortunately, Don and Teresa found instructions from Roy conveniently on the work surface inside the flip top desk where Roy took care of the finances. And with the help of Loraine and Janice, they got things under control.

Loraine's vivid memory of her Mom and Dad riding in the car together with Kathryn sitting as close as possible to Roy made her smile. Some of her high school friends would swoon at how romantic her parents still were after so many years of marriage. Now, she was warmed by the knowledge that she had been blessed with parents who were still in love with each other and set a good example for their children about how marriage should be. She never saw or heard them argue. When there were disagreements, one of them would walk away until sometime later when the children couldn't hear. Home was a place of love, safety and sharing.

Within a few weeks after Roy's death, Kathryn sold their home and moved to Roswell from southeast Atlanta because she needed a ride to and from work. Her office had moved to the Roswell area and one of her close friends at work lived near Roswell and offered to be her transportation each day. Moving day was emotional for Kathryn. She was leaving her home that she and Roy had loved. All her furniture would not fit into the apartment she

185

rented. Sentimental items were sold or parsed out to grandchildren. She was starting over again. The remarkable thing was that Kathryn did not feel sorry for herself. She was unsure about some things and she just didn't want to participate in other things, but she lived her life as best she could without complaint or asking "why me". Somewhere along the way she had shed the unworthiness from her outlook. She was thankful for her children and grandchildren and enjoyed the time they spent with her. She approached each opportunity offered to her with enthusiasm.

With her children's encouragement, she took driving lessons and passed the driving exam. However, driving for the first time at age 60 was never comfortable for her. She mapped out a course from her apartment where she could drive to the hairdresser and grocery store each weekend taking only right turns. But when she retired she didn't try to improve her comfort as a driver and stayed in her apartment all the time except for her weekend trips for groceries and hair appointments.

Loraine remembered the day they moved her from that small apartment in Roswell to an apartment in the same complex where Loraine and the boys lived in Gainesville, so she would be close to Loraine and her sons. Being a single mom, left Loraine with daily responsibilities of getting the boys to and from school and to all of the extra-curricular activities after school while working a full-time job. She could use Kathryn's new driving skills to help with those duties.

Loraine felt it would give Kathryn something to look forward to each day and give her a feeling of being needed. She had been correct in her assumption. Kathryn immediately rose out of her depression since her retirement and, not only, immersed herself in her new challenge, but accompanied Loraine to Jeff's Friday night football games the following years. Her keen wit returned and she blossomed with the closeness of Loraine and sons.

Loraine had been conflicted with the decision to encourage Kathryn to move away from her beloved Atlanta because she knew how much Kathryn loved the city. But in the months since her retirement at age 62, she had become reclusive.

Gainesville was a much smaller town and traffic was slow and sparse in those years. Kathryn began to feel comfortable driving the ten or twelve miles from her apartment to the schools. The boys loved having their grandmother pick them up and shared their days' events with her. She was back with family and began to flourish during those years. She even accepted the challenge to be a receptionist in a new business Loraine started. She enjoyed meeting the clients and she always had a smile and positive comment to all the customers. True to her unselfish nature, she refused any pay for the hours she worked. For a struggling new business, this was a God-send.

Things began to become difficult when a year after Loraine and Billy married they bought a house and moved five miles from the apartments. Loraine struggled with memories of how Kathryn adjusted to each change in her life with her sweet nature and supportive words for each family member. She was always available to listen to her children's problems and never offered advice unless asked for. She would respond that she would pray for them and told them to pray about the situation too. She would end the conversation with her statement that, "God will take care of you and this situation. Just ask for his help."

46.

Janice and her daughter, Deborah arrived early afternoon. As the grandchildren began to arrive at the hospital, it was apparent that the small strokes Kathryn had been having over the past few years had finally developed into a major stroke. Kathryn never opened her eyes again. The doctors recommended that she be placed under Hospice care in the hospital. She had shown no signs of the infection she had developed in the rehab center. Therefore, she met the medical criteria to remain under hospital hospice staff.

Kathryn was not left alone by family until she was greeted by her comforting angel and taken to be with Jesus. Jeff, who had a special love for Kathryn, sat by her bed for hours, working on his computer and playing 40's music which was the music of her youth. Everyone felt it comforted her. The nursing staff told the family that even though she was non-responsive, she could still hear. Kevin, who shared Kathryn's dry sense of humor and his own special love for her, came into town and comforted Loraine by never leaving Kathryn's room. Their California son, Jeff, flew home to share in the grief Loraine went through and spent the night on the floor in Kathryn's room along with Kevin and Loraine, Janice and Deborah. Loraine was surrounded by the love of her three sons.

Don and Teresa came. All three siblings were there to show their love for their Mother.

They shared happy memories of their life with Kathryn and Roy. Stories of Kathryn's later years brought laughter to the group. Her life-long self-consciousness never interfered with her ability to make fun of herself for all the crazy things that senior adults do. Special times spent with each family member were shared and everyone felt her presence.

Occasionally, a stray tear would slowly caress Kathryn's face. Even though the nurses said that everyone who went through this process did the same thing, Loraine felt it was her way of saying goodbye. With the last few muted breaths, Loraine noticed a bright light at the foot of the hospital bed. In the midst of the light a form appeared and she heard the angel say, "Don't be afraid. I'll be with you all the way."

Loraine knew Kathryn was with God now.

Made in the USA
Lexington, KY
13 August 2017